# The Nothing Club

# The Nothing Club

**CATHY BEVERIDGE**

Ronsdale Press

THE NOTHING CLUB
Copyright © 2025 Cathy Beveridge

All rights reserved, including those for text and data mining, A.I. training, and similar technologies. No part of this publication may be reproduced, stored in a retrieval system, or transmitted, in any form or by any means, without prior written permission of the publisher, or, in Canada, in the case of photocopying or other reprographic copying, a licence from Access Copyright (the Canadian Copyright Licensing Agency).

RONSDALE PRESS
125A – 1030 Denman Street, Vancouver, B.C. Canada V6G 2M6
www.ronsdalepress.com

Book Design: Derek von Essen
Cover Design: David Lester
Editor: Robyn So

Ronsdale Press wishes to thank the following for their support of its publishing program: the Canada Council for the Arts, the Government of Canada, the British Columbia Arts Council, and the Province of British Columbia through the British Columbia Book Publishing Tax Credit program.

Library and Archives Canada Cataloguing in Publication

Title: The Nothing Club / Cathy Beveridge.
Names: Beveridge, Cathy, author.
Identifiers: Canadiana (print) 2024051856X | Canadiana (ebook) 20240518578 | ISBN 9781553807285
  (softcover) | ISBN 9781553807292 (EPUB)
Subjects: LCGFT: Novels.
Classification: LCC PS8553.E897 N68 2025 | DDC C813/.6—dc23

At Ronsdale Press we are committed to protecting the environment. To this end we are working with Canopy and printers to phase out our use of paper produced from ancient forests. This book is one step towards that goal.

Printed in Canada

For my grandchildren, Ethan, Emily and Logan.
May you always fall upwards.

ACKNOWLEDGEMENTS

This novel was inspired by Richard Rohr's teachings, and numerous discussions about spirituality, judgement and forgiveness with my close friends Wendy, Gwen and Kelly, as well as my own journey in that regard. I am also grateful to my partner Jeff for his support and encouragement, to my daughter Michelle for reading multiple versions of this manuscript, to my editor Robyn So for her insights and expertise, and to the staff at Ronsdale Press for their engagement and feedback throughout the publishing process.

# PROLOGUE

Forgiving others is one thing but forgiving yourself after you've hurt someone — well that's a whole different matter. Especially when you meant to hurt. I mean it should be easier in theory. You just acknowledge what you've done wrong, feel remorseful, repent and apologize to yourself. And then you forgive yourself! Easy-peasy, except it's not! It's downright impossible. Because when others forgive you, they don't know the devious thoughts you had at the moment of your transgression. But you know, and when you try to forgive yourself, you still know. And no apology or penance is going to eradicate that knowledge . . . so you're stuck. With all the guilt that goes with not being forgiven! But you're also stuck with the idea that it's permanent. You're going to carry that guilt like a heavy backpack full of useless stuff forever. Unless you find a way to do the impossible.

# CHAPTER 1

It's sweltering when I stumble into the kitchen after work, ravenous for anything but cinnamon doughnuts. That's because I spend my days working at one of those tiny doughnut shops — pouring, flipping, scooping sugar-and-cinnamon–coated doughnuts into greasy paper bags and handing them to drooling children. A pot of chili bubbles on the stove even though it's got to be 30 degrees outside. Mom is on the phone, and I can hear Charlotte and her friend Peter playing in the front room. I dish up a bowl of kidney beans etc., suitable for a fifteen-year-old guy with two hollow legs — as my mother likes to say — grab a bun, tear it in half and dunk it in my bowl. There is a garden salad in the fridge, but vegetables and I don't see eye to eye, except for potatoes. I snicker at my own joke then chow down as Mom strides into the room, the phone tucked into her shoulder. She is in her fraud buster uniform — black sweats and a cherry red T-shirt. She works for the Better Business Bureau from her home office and is obviously on hold.

Mom runs her fingers through her short reddish-brown curls and adjusts the papers in her free hand. "How was work, Grady?"

"I'm going to stay at Will's tonight," I say at the same time.

"Good, good, I bet you were busy," she replies.

I study the dark bags under her preoccupied eyes. She tries but she's hardly ever in the present moment. There's a lot to do in the house and yard now, and she's almost always tired. That can be advantageous sometimes. "His cousin's in town from Kelowna," I answer without hesitation.

She inclines her head to hear some automated receptionist. "Well, it is the busiest time of the year. Everyone loves those little doughnuts."

"Tyler," I say, continuing to test out my potential advantage.

"And it's great experience. Looks good on a resumé too." She punches a number into the phone.

It looks like I have some latitude. "He brought fireworks," I add with an agreeable intonation.

"Fireworks!" She clicks the phone off.

So much for my theory.

"Those are illegal in the city without a permit."

"Yeah, yeah, I know. I just said he brought them, not that we were going to set them off." As I say it, I wonder if that isn't a bit like going to *just look* at puppies.

Mom's hazel eyes continue to scrutinize me. "Well, don't you boys go getting into trouble! And you have to be home by eleven tomorrow morning. I have an appointment, and you need to keep an eye on Charlotte."

"Okay," I agree begrudgingly. "But I work at four fifteen, so you had better be back before then."

"Deal," she says and redials.

Will opens the front door before I can knock. "Did you know that male Muscovy ducks' penises are shaped like corkscrews?" he asks as I step into the foyer.

"Uh, can't say I did," I reply, swallowing the greeting on my lips. "Is that true?"

"Yep, I bet the females love it." Will heads down the hallway. I try to picture Muscovy ducks doing it with corkscrewed penises while I struggle out of my high-tops.

Will lives in a 4,000-square-foot mansion even though there's just him and his parents. His dad's a big oil exec and gone most of the time so Will doesn't see him very often. He sees the butler, Maurice, quite a bit though, and so does his mother, but that's another story that we don't talk about. They brought Maurice back with them from Brunei, where they lived for six years when his dad was really raking in the money.

Maurice greets me with a slight bow. "Master Grady, how nice to see you." He reaches for my backpack, and I hand it over.

"Hey, Maurice," I say. Maurice is dressed in a pristine, white button-down shirt and black dress pants. His hair is well-coiffed, and he looks quite distinguished.

I half-slide down the polished floors in my socks, hang a right and jump down the two steps into the games room, where Will is leaning against the pool table. A tall, ripped kid with an impressive tan is racking up the balls. Will's cousin.

"Hey," he says, glancing up with chestnut brown eyes from beneath a mop of blond hair and looking like he should be on a billboard for underwear.

"Hey, I'm Grady."

"Tyler," Mr. Underwear replies. "You can play the winner."

I watch Tyler break, then glide around the table. He is soundless and light on his feet and his limbs move like water flowing. Will, on the other hand, clunks about the room, holding his cue like a club. I am not surprised when Tyler sinks the last ball.

"Boys!" Will's mom's voice reaches us through the intercom.

"Yeah, Mom."

"I have a charity function tonight and Maurice is driving me. I'll be late."

"Okay," we all call in unison.

"Perfect," Tyler says, laying down the cue and glancing out the window where the sun is starting to drop. "We have just enough time to set up the fireworks before dark." I glance at Will, but Tyler's statement is obviously not an invitation for discussion. Will shrugs and I relax. What harm can it do? A beautiful summer night sky is about to become a little brighter.

The fireworks consist of three bundles of Roman candles covered in shiny purple paper. Tyler hands each of us one and we head out into the backyard. Will's house overlooks a large natural off-leash dog area that consists of rolling hills, saskatoon berry bushes and meandering wood-chip trails that lead from the cliffs to the river. Built so that Will's dad can see the mountains he never actually gets to, the house stands high on the hill above the park, which is full of swaying grasses, thistles and wild rose bushes. Will's gardener, armed with a whipper-snapper and Roundup, fights a constant battle to keep the lawn looking like a putting green and to know at all times where the wild things are.

Tyler leads the way to the iron gate at the back of the yard, and we slip into a mass of grasses, burrs and mosquitoes. "Where are you thinking of setting them off?" asks Will.

I glance sideways at him as he swats at the insects that plague him more than anyone I have ever met. As a result, Tyler and I are virtually free of bugs buzzing around us. I slap a mosquito that has landed on the back of Will's arm and blood splatters in the shape of an ink blot. For a moment, I wonder how much blood a tiny insect can hold, but my reverie is interrupted by Tyler, who is striding towards a grassy plateau partway down the hill.

"Over here!" he exclaims, tramping through the wind-bowed grass. A dirt trail winds its way through the valley below but quickly drops beneath the crest of the hill, leaving us almost invisible to anyone in the park.

Will joins me on the plateau, his long fine hair whipping over his glasses. "It's pretty windy out here," he tells Tyler. "It would be better to find a more sheltered space." We turn in a tight circle, surveying the terrain, but this is the only relatively flat spot in the whole valley unless we head to the bottom where the bike paths run.

"It'll work," says Tyler. The sun is clinging to the horizon, but we know its grip is tenuous. In a matter of minutes, it will slip over the edge into tomorrow.

"How do you work these things?" asks Will, turning the Roman candle upside down and using it to shoo mosquitoes away.

"You light 'em and let 'em go," says Tyler. He kneels at the edge of the knoll. "Help me clear a spot down to the dirt, and then we'll dig them in so they stand up."

"Aren't we supposed to have a rack?" I ask.

"You can just stand them in the dirt."

We pull at the heat-stricken grass, tearing it free then using our fingers to dig out the roots and level the dusty dirt. Once we have cleared a sizable patch, we press the ends of the Roman candles into the ground, piling the soil up around their bases to hold them in place. They teeter and totter but do not fall down. Twilight has blanketed the hill, but a halo of sunset remains, so we sit beside the fireworks and wait out the sky.

"Did you know that Dr. Mengele, a Nazi doctor, experimented on fifteen thousand sets of twins during the war?" says Will.

I wonder if any of the neurons in Will's brain follow a pattern and from the look in Tyler's eye, so does he. But Will is oblivious to our voiceless concerns. "The guy was so warped that he extracted hearts and stomachs from one twin without anesthetic, then killed the other one immediately to conduct comparative autopsies."

My jaw tightens instinctively. I am hoping it will get dark quickly. Natural darkness is easier to deal with than human darkness.

"I heard about him," says Tyler. "The Angel of Death. He used to do selections at the concentration camps — left you die, right you live. Or was it right you die, left you live?"

"My dad saw those crematoriums. He said they look like human pizza ovens," Will responds.

My stomach heaves and I point at the sky. "It'll be dark soon. Let's shoot these things," I say, even though a big part of me just wants to head home and eat marmalade toast at Mom's table with my little sister.

Tyler extracts a lighter from his pocket and I stare in amazement. The Roman candles don't have huge fuses on them, and that little device isn't going to give us much time to light all three and retreat. "Are we going to send them off one by one?" I ask.

"No way!" says Will. "We'd attract too much attention to ourselves. All three at once."

Tyler grins, tucks his blowing curls behind his ear and flicks the lighter. The flame is immediately extinguished by the wind. He flicks it again, but it stays lit only a brief moment before being blown out. "Come here," Tyler instructs us. "I need a windbreak."

I realize that I have slowly been backing away from the fireworks. The last thing I really want to do is stand above the Roman candles while they're lit, but on Tyler's order, I move reluctantly towards them.

"I'll light them fast, and then we run like hell towards that stand of trees," he says, pointing uphill to his left. Will and I nod, and I can feel my heartbeat in my temples. Tyler bends down and Will and I shelter the flame. One fuse lit, then two . . . I turn and head for the trees.

"What the . . . ?" Tyler screams and when I look back both fuses are out, extinguished by the wind.

"I-I, uh, thought you had all three there," I lie. I return but now there is an even bigger issue. The two fuses have burnt down some. They'll go faster when lit.

"Light the third one first," suggests Will and I can see by the perspiration on his forehead that he's thinking the same thing I am.

"Like duh," says Tyler. "One, two . . ."

Will grabs my wrist and holds me there.

". . . three!"

We run for cover, dive into the trees and look back. A thin wisp of smoke rises into the twilight.

"Looks like it's too windy," I say, relieved.

Tyler retraces his steps, and we follow. One of the candles lies on its side, half-obscured by the grass. "We'll wait for a lull," he says determinedly. The wind gusts, defying his words, and suddenly a flame leaps in the grass. "Shit! It's still burning."

We stand rooted to the spot for a moment. Then Will takes off his jacket to beat the flame, but I grab him and yank him away. "What if it goes off?"

Tyler stands on his tiptoes, looking from me to the flame dancing over the grasses. Then he bolts towards the upscale condos that separate us from Will's house.

**THE NOTHING CLUB**

We follow, racing past a driveway where two little girls are skipping rope. "We have to call the fire department," I gasp.

I stop and pull my cell phone from my pocket, but Tyler smacks it from my hand. "Don't be an idiot," he says. "You'll incriminate us."

Don't we deserve to be incriminated? I pick my phone up off the grass, my mind swirling.

"Hey," Tyler calls to the blond girl with her hair in pigtails. "We need your help."

She regards him suspiciously. The skipping rope droops to the concrete.

"Run inside and tell your parents there's a grass fire behind your house. It's really important."

The little skipper's eyes widen. "For real?"

Tyler nods. "Yeah. They need to call the fire department."

Her rosy pink lips form a perfect O and she races for the door. Her friend hurries after her. As soon as they have disappeared from view, a blast rockets through the air and light shoots upwards. We bolt towards Will's. The smell of smoke is now distinctly discernible as we reach the back deck. Tyler laughs aloud.

But all I can do is hope that the fire trucks hurry. It's all I will allow myself to think about. Soon the air fills with human cries.

"Let's go back," urges Will.

Tyler studies both of us. "You got any ball caps?" he asks Will. We enter the empty house, and Tyler instructs us to grab jackets. I haven't brought one, so I slip Will's hockey jacket on. *Hawks* reads the red logo across my back. I choose a yellow ABC *Petroleum* cap and survey the other guys. Tyler adds his sunglasses, and Will tucks his hair under his Toronto Blue Jays baseball hat. Tyler nods in approval and leads the way back towards the fire.

People hurry in the same direction, moms carrying yappy dogs, dads with their shirt sleeves rolled up. Around the corner, a wave of flame buffets the wind. Two men are trying to snuff it out with their coats. My heart leaps in my chest. The other Roman candles — someone should warn them!

"Water!" calls a man from the yard of a condo. He is dragging a long hose towards the fire, and the men fighting the flames turn and run to help him. It's a good thing because it is at that moment that another Roman candle explodes. Sparks sizzle and shoot in all directions. The crowd gasps.

I feel nauseous. Perspiration trickles down my forehead and my feet stick.

"Get out of here!" screams one of the men, motioning at the crowd. "Now!"

Sirens scream in the street and the crowd turns towards the fire trucks. I spin sideways, away from Will and Tyler, stumbling back against the rough siding of the condo. Boom! Another explosion rocks the hillside, and the firefighters are there now, barking orders, evacuating the area. "Let's go, son," one tells me, and I look up, hoping for a brief moment, but he is a stranger. My feet stumble onto the pavement. I head home, a jumble of stupidity, guilt and trepidation.

It takes twenty-four hours for the cops to come around. Mom hears about the fire in the evening, but when she asks me if it's near Will's, I lie and tell her I'm not sure, but that I heard it really scarred the hillside and it's a real shame — lots of damage to the environment due to those tinder-dry grasses — a real pity. Then she gives me her investigator look, and I tell her I have to work early, even before the doughnut shop opens.

The officers show up while I'm changing. As soon as I see the uniforms, I know I'm busted. The cops are both youngish fellows with enormous hands. My palms sweat and before anyone asks, I'm blurting out the whole story, only they already know it. They've already been to Will's place and, well, it was an open and shut case really. The little skipping girls have great futures as private investigators.

The cops take me down to the station. I ask about Will, but apparently, his father's lawyer is dealing with stuff on behalf of him and his cousin. And they wonder why poor folks figure more prominently in the crime stats! Not that we're super poor, but by comparison to Will, we're destitute. Because it's my first offence, and because I sweat profusely and almost break into tears when I apologize, the charges are dropped. Instead, I get community service work, and I can still work for real. My knees tremble as I leave with my mother.

She waits until we are in the car before she says the thing I've dreaded most. "Your father," she starts, her words dripping with disappointment, "would have been appalled." Her head shakes. "A fire, of all things. As if you don't understand the damage a fire can do." Her eyes tear up and I fight to keep the hearse closed. "Fires take lives, Grady. You know that."

If only I didn't.

# CHAPTER 2

I'm assigned to community service work, to be supervised by the maintenance man, Reg, at the Glenmeadows Community Centre throughout July and August. The centre is an older wooden building with a fresh coat of sea glass green paint. Inside is a gym, a few conference rooms and an office. It's nothing special except for the massive row of poplars that borders its grounds, half-hiding an outdoor courtyard and swimming pool. There is something peaceful about the greenery and gardens surrounding a silent pool. A note on the office door directs me across the lawns to the shed, a plain structure near the playground, from which a weathered man emerges as I arrive. Reg doesn't seem to notice the shame etched on my features. "You must be Grady," he says instead, rubbing the stubble on his cheeks and chin.

"Yeah, I'm starting community service, but I guess you know that . . . as well as why I'm here." I figure it's easier just to be upfront about stuff.

"Here," replies Reg. He hands me a broom and asks me to brush the freshly cut grass and debris from the courtyard, then disappears into the office. I drop my backpack next to some cement blocks. The courtyard serves as a basketball court and is flanked by two nets. I start brushing in one corner, trying to sweep away the past. At first it feels awkward, but soon the rhythm of the brush takes over and by the time Reg returns, the courtyard is swept clean. I'd put him around fifty or so, medium height, muscular build with a swath of thick carbon-black hair that looks like it's dyed, except he doesn't strike me as the dyeing type. Maybe it's just because the knees of his jeans are covered in dirt, but there's a grounded, down-to-earth feel to the guy. Kind of safe. He smiles, then motions for me to join him.

I pick up my pack and follow him towards a vegetable garden that he's obviously expanding. Something dark green has gone to seed, and something else a lighter shade of green is threatening to take over the bean-shaped things. I'm not a big plant guy.

A shovel teeters, stuck in the newly broken ground. Reg pulls it free and carries it to an adjacent flower bed. "Been trying all spring to get rid of this quack grass, but I'm losing the battle." He stands in front of a clump of long grasses, then steps on the shovel. Its blade pierces the earth, loosening the dirt. Reaching for one long shoot, he slides his tanned hand down its stem and gently pulls its roots free. Three short ones emerge followed by one longer tubular root. "Their roots run underground," explains Reg. "This piece here, it's probably connected to that one over there." He points at another wide blade of quack grass near another clump of white flowers.

I nod and look up to find Reg studying me. Probably trying to figure out how such a decent-looking kid fell off the straight and narrow. I brace myself for the questions, admonitions, the inevitable lecture I deserve.

"Well, shall we test my theory?" he asks. He hands me the shovel. I dig its tip beneath the clump of quack grass about three metres away from Reg's and jiggle the handle. Then I reach down and extract the roots. Sure enough one long root runs in Reg's direction. I tug my end gently and Reg does the same from his side. Suddenly the root springs loose from the dirt, leaving us connected by one long unbroken thread.

He looks at me expectantly, and that's when I realize that I am missing something. "Everything is connected," he says, helping me out this time. I get the feeling that I will have to extract my own message next time around.

"Sure," I say my cheeks burning. How can this chill gardener be connected to a numbskull like me?

He gestures at the nearby shed. "You can leave your backpack in there. If anyone comes around, Walter will let us know."

"Walter?"

"Mmm," says Reg, picking up his shovel and heading back to the vegetable garden.

Walter turns out to be the oldest, drooliest, deafest chocolate lab that ever existed. He lays in a patch of shade just inside the open door, thumps his tail on the hard wooden floor and pants. "Hey boy," I say rubbing his ears. I dump my pack on the bench and Walter sniffs. "It's a ham sandwich and if you leave it alone, I'll share at lunch," I tell him. Walter drools as I hang my backpack on a hook, a dog-induced happiness filling my gut. I've tried to explain that feeling to my mother every time I try to talk her into getting a dog — about four times a week — but she doesn't get it. My dad did.

Reg does too. "Not only does Walter speak human, but he's fluent in cat and squirrel," he informs me as he checks in on me later, back at the garden.

I believe it. I continue weeding, wondering why it's called quack grass, but there are no ducks around to ask. Reg stops by about an hour later and hands me a cold bottle of water. "Thanks," I say, guzzling half. He drinks from his, and I watch the bubbles fizzle from his lips to the water's surface. "So, don't you even want to know what I did?" I ask finally. I am ready to be condemned; I deserve to be condemned.

"There's nothing to keep you from talking to the daisies," he tells me, motioning at the white petals surrounded by bees. He takes his leave as the sun burns a hole in the clouds. "Washroom's in the pool building," Reg calls over his shoulder. "There's a concession in there too." He saunters away. "Lunch is when you take it, and it lasts an hour."

I take it at 12:15 but there's no sign of Reg. I hope they aren't paying him for lunchtime supervision. I settle into the shade and wonder what Will is up to. I'm guessing he's not weeding flower beds in oppressive heat. I groan. Just two more months to go! Walter noses my elbow, waiting patiently for my crusts and a mustard-slathered piece of ham. When we've both eaten, I dig a toonie out of my shorts pocket and head to the concession stand at the pool. A petite, green-eyed girl with dark brown hair peers up at me over lilac-rimmed glasses. She doesn't ask me what I want, but I order a Rocket and toss my toonie on the counter. She passes me the frozen treat without looking up. "Thanks," I whisper, unsure of why I've whispered. She glances at me, and I try to figure out how old she is. Maybe my age? I wonder what her name is, or if she even has one.

"Do you have a name?" I ask, then tacitly acknowledge the stupidity of the question.

"Catherine," she whispers, but doesn't ask me mine.

Reg believes that you ought to "shovel while the sun shines" so basically, I spend my time weeding flower beds, digging gardens and cutting grass during the day, then working at the doughnut stand at night. By Wednesday my skin is baked a doughnut shade of brown, and I am looking forward to a night off. I am hoping to see Will before he gets deported to some camp in Switzerland on Friday, where his community service work consists of teaching kids to design video games in the Alps. Connections are so nice. My mother on the other hand is still setting off her own fireworks whenever I come into view, so I know a visit to Will is out of the question.

Friday, I eat lunch with Walter, then go buy a Freezie from the I-Wish-I-Were-Invisible girl. Ambling back to the shed, I suddenly realize there is a figure between me and my destination. A wave of black energy runs across me, and I immediately detour around the side of a large dumpster where she can't see me, but I can see her.

I have never seen so many tattoos on a single slim body in my life. A dragon slithers down her left arm, its curved talons extending to her middle finger. She wears jeans slit at the knees and flip-flops; even her heels are coloured green and red and blue, although I can't make out the design. She's got an Asian look about her, and only her face and a portion of her throat visible above her T-shirt are not tattooed. I crouch behind the dumpster. With her fingers dug into her jean pockets and one hip jutting forward, she wears attitude. Glistening smooth hair hangs straight to her shoulders, half-obscuring one eye and dark pierced lips. Defiance oozes from her and that is the energy that surrounds me now, dark and intimidating. I remain where I am.

She enters the shed, then re-emerges when she discovers it empty. Walter lies in a shady patch of grass. His tail thumps quietly and as she bends down beside him, her energy suddenly softens. "Hey boy," she says so softly that I can barely hear her. Folding her legs neatly under her, she sits cross-legged beside the dog. Then suddenly her arms encircle Walter, drawing him to her in a hug.

The dark is gone and in its place is only vulnerability. Now I'm really stuck next to the dumpster. I can't invade that place. Besides, I doubt that *Tattoo Girl* would want me to know she goes there. I finish my Freezie and sit, wondering what she's done to deserve community service. A squirrel stirs in the tree above her, and she stands and watches it. Now's as good a time as any. I stride towards the shed, feeling her black curtain of energy draw solidly back into place.

"Where's Reg?" she asks in a voice that clearly belongs somewhere on the streets after dark. Tattoo Girl's eyes bore a hole in my forehead.

"Not here." I wonder if he knew she was coming today, and if so, why he didn't stick around.

"So, when's he gonna be here?" There is a cultivated edge in her voice, a deliberate posturing in her stance.

"He'll be back around one."

"Which is?" she demands.

I glance up at her puzzled. "Which is . . . ?" I repeat.

"The time, nimrod."

"Ten minutes." I brush past her and pet Walter. "You here for community service work . . ." I hesitate then add, "too?"

She looks up, lifting momentarily the veil she wears so convincingly, then drops it again. "You don't look like the delinquent type," she says, giving me the once over. "They'd kill you on the streets."

I shrug. "Some fireworks got outta control. Lit the park on fire."

"Frickin' brilliant!" she snorts.

"And you?"

"They got nothing on me," she declares.

We sit in silence and her urge to escape is palpable.

Instead, she pulls Reg's notepad off the bench, flips past his lists and reminders and begins to draw.

I tilt my head, angling for a better look until she glares at me accusingly.

"Can I see?" I ask as the sketch rapidly takes shape.

She inclines it towards me. A dying lion trampled by an antelope, an expression of revenge on its delicate features. I wonder who the lion in her life is. "You do your own designs?" I ask, motioning towards her inked arms.

"So what if I do?"

"They're good," I say quickly. "Very good."

"I can do one for you," she offers cockily. "And a buddy of mine could tattoo you if you aren't too much of a wuss."

I shake my head and laugh. "I'm a total wuss when it comes to needles." Besides, I know that if I get a tattoo, my mother will do her Roman candle imitation. Tattoo Girl continues to sketch, momentarily confused by my honest cowardice. I pluck up my courage. "I'm Grady, by the way."

She doesn't look up. "Margaret."

"Margaret!" I spit the name out of the side of my mouth. "Right!" She looks pissed. "You just do not seem like a Margaret."

"I think I know my own name."

I raise my hands in mock surrender. "Okay then, Margar-et." I return to petting Walter, rubbing his ears and nose gently as she draws.

"Nobody calls me that," she admits after a bit. "At least not on the street."

I wait but she doesn't go on. Then I gesture towards the dog. "And this is Walter."

She pats the dog's head, then rubs his ears. "Nice to meet you, Walter boy," she says. "I'm Tattoo Girl."

I almost laugh aloud.

Reg puts her to work sorting seed packets and cleaning out the shed, taking the exact same interest in her *crime* as he did in mine. Nil! I wonder if he's shared any moments of wisdom, but somehow, I have the feeling that it's too early with Tattoo Girl. She wears attitude in layers and by the end of the day, I find myself wondering if it's not tattooed on permanently. I'll have to wait until Monday to find out.

Tattoo Girl's defiance is tightly drawn around her after the weekend. I emerge from the men's change room at the pool just before ten o'clock, as she arrives at the concession. "A Creamsicle," she demands of Catherine, pushing her bottom lip with its silver ring forward. "And what say I pay you for one and you make it two." Catherine turns bright red but does not respond. Her slender fingers pick up the toonie as Tattoo Girl slams her tattooed claws down on top of them. "You deaf?" Catherine shakes her head, and I swear her shoulders tremble. "And don't wear lilac deodorant tomorrow. I hate lilacs."

Tattoo Girl's talons scrape across the counter as Catherine digs two Creamsicles out of the freezer, passes them over and shrinks backwards. I press forward and Tattoo Girl brushes past me with a look of indifference that must have taken years to perfect.

"A Rocket, please," I say, approaching the concession and passing Catherine a five-dollar bill. "And keep the change."

"You-you don't have to do that," she says, her lips moving so quickly she seems to be part of a fast-forward movie.

It's the first time she's spoken to me, and I am taken aback by the richness of her voice. "It's okay. Keep the change."

"I have money. Money's not the issue." Her voice breaks and I lean forward instinctively, feeling a need to comfort her with absolutely no idea how to do so. She spits at me in a whisper. "She'll do this every day now. Every single day."

Her truth makes me shudder. "No, she won't," I promise Catherine. "I'll make sure she doesn't." She gives me such a sincere look of skepticism and gratitude then that I bind myself further to my foolish promise. I'm determined to keep it too, only by the time I reach the shed, Free Throw has arrived, and everything has changed.

## CHAPTER 3

His T-shirt is soaked with sweat. "Sorry I'm late," Free Throw proclaims. "Antoine had a fever, and Natasha lost a shoe, so I missed the bus. I thought it might be faster if I ran." He pauses as we stare incoherently at him, then explains, "I've got eight brothers and sisters."

"Never mind," Reg tells him. "It's good to see you."

Tattoo Girl lets out a loud guffaw. "You mean I can be late if I just happen to lose a shoe?"

Reg ignores her. We are cleaning out a storage room adjoining the community centre's gym.

"By the way, I think I feel a fever coming on, Reginald." Tattoo Girl puts a hand on her forehead and lets her knees buckle, sinking onto a dusty gym mat.

"Isn't your name Reg?" asks Free Throw. Reg nods and I realize that there is something unnaturally simple about Free Throw. At 195 centimetres, with bronze skin and teeth the colour of alabaster, his presence seems to lighten the room. He turns to Tattoo Girl. "If his name's not Reginald, you shouldn't call him that."

"What, you wanna be my mother now?" she snaps.

Free Throw's laugh is pure magic. It brushes the cobwebs

in the corners of the room and effortlessly tightrope walks across the tension. He sweeps a giant hand the length of his long body. "Do I look like your mama?" he asks with so much frank innocence that I have to laugh.

At lunch, Tattoo Girl disappears. I dig into my lunch bag and pull out two roast beef buns. I have taken to making two because Walter usually eats half of one. The dog is lying on his side, and Free Throw's massive hands move over Walter's fur in what could only be called a caress. I am about to tear the second bun in half for Walter when I realize that Free Throw doesn't have a lunch. "Damn," I say, "I told my mom not to pack me two. You wouldn't be into roast beef, would you, man? I have to work tonight, and it'll be bad by the time I get home."

Free Throw accepts it graciously. I look at his almost skeletal frame and try to guess how much food he can pack away. He opens his mouth to take a bite, then stops, tears off a chunk of the sandwich and offers it to Walter.

I chuckle. "That dog's gonna get fat with both of us here."

Free Throw chows down on the bun, a mustard smile spreading across his cheeks. "Where's he live?" he asks, stroking Walter's silky ears.

"There's a house not far away." I noticed it tucked behind a tall hedge the other day. A fancy house, with a garden — a magazine-cover type house. "I'm guessing he spends his nights there and his days here." Not a bad life for a dog, or a human for that matter. Walter's tail wags as if in confirmation, and Free Throw's giant hands massage his coat. "Do you have a dog?" I ask.

Free Throw shakes his head. "Mom says there's too many of us already."

I contemplate that as I chew. He could conceivably come from a family of ten. That's wild. "You like having so many brothers and sisters?"

"Sometimes. But I have to look after them lots."

I think about my little sister and how much I resent having to babysit her on the odd occasion when Mom's out. "Yeah, I get it," I tell him. "So, who's looking after them while you're here?" It's the first time I've alluded to the question of what's landed Free Throw at the community centre under Reg's supervision, and I wonder if I am on shaky ground.

"My auntie."

"What'd you do anyway, Free Throw?" I blurt out, curiosity overcoming discretion. Immediately, I regret doing so. "You don't . . ."

"Break and enter."

"Break and enter?" This is far more serious than I'd imagined.

"I smashed the window of an old warehouse."

"Really?"

"Yep, it was stupid. The kitten, she didn't even make it."

I gulp down the chunk of granola bar I've bitten off, then tear a piece off the remaining bar and hand it to him. "You mean you broke into a warehouse to rescue a kitten, and it died?"

Free Throw's dark brown eyes turn wistful. "She was too weak. I should have done it days before."

"And they gave you community service for that?"

He shrugs. "Here I am."

I punch his lean arm, not knowing what to say or do.

"Oh pulease," cuts in Tattoo Girl, stomping into the shed. She grabs cash from her jacket pocket and heads towards the pool.

"You going to the concession?" I leap to my feet, recalling my promise to Catherine. "Why don't I come with you?"

"Because I'm going alone." She storms out of the shed, and I hesitate.

"What just went down?" asks Free Throw, joining me at the door.

**THE NOTHING CLUB**            31

"She pays for one and demands two."

"That girl's got no respect."

I recall her with Walter when she thought she was unseen. "She's not as bad as she seems," I say, although even I have to admit that I don't sound overly convincing. But Free Throw is on the move, overtaking Tattoo Girl with long, rapid strides. Man, the guy can accelerate. I race after them.

"What is this? A concession booth party?" snarls Tattoo Girl when we all arrive together.

"Hello," says Free Throw, waving at Catherine over Tattoo Girl's head. "I'm Free Throw."

"Catherine," mumbles Catherine, each syllable of her name dripping with discomfort. She tucks her lilac-coloured handbag beneath her chair.

"You run the concession?"

Catherine nods, her body pulled away from Tattoo Girl, who's leaning menacingly across the counter.

"These are my friends Grady and Tattoo Girl." Free Throw gestures behind the concession. "And this is my new friend, Catherine."

Tattoo Girl rolls her eyes. "You can't be for real!" She yanks on her hair as if to rip it from her head. Her dragon slithers sideways across the counter. "Okay," she declares, glaring at Free Throw. "I pay for what I buy. And you stop with the friendly giant stuff!"

Without warning, Free Throw wraps his arms around her and lifts her into the air. I wonder if he's going to get a knee to the groin, but Tattoo Girl just dangles for a moment, sputters, then turns away. I think I see the hint of a smile.

It's hard not to smile when Free Throw's around. He's just so damn happy all the time. As we reach the courtyard, I grab a basketball and pass it to him. "Do you play?"

"Duh!" says Tattoo Girl. "Let's see. His name is Free Throw."

Free Throw grins. "Actually," he tells her, bouncing the ball to me and striding out onto the court, "I got that name in grade six. I missed a hundred free throws in a row at a school competition. I think it was a school record."

"Really?" I ask, shooting and sinking the ball. "That's impressive."

"Yeah! And I was actually trying," he admits. "I shoot with my little brother sometimes. He's way better than me."

I dribble the ball, wondering when the last time I played with my little sister was. A wave of guilt rolls over me. Just one more sin to add to my list. "Well, if basketball's not your thing, then you ought to try running. You can really motor," I tell him.

"I won the city championships in the four-hundred-metre race last spring," he says with a shy smile. I hit him with a bounce pass and he shoots. The basketball arcs through the air and swishes through the hoop. "Time to quit," he says laughing.

"What I don't get," says Tattoo Girl to Free Throw on Thursday as we paint the conference room walls, "is why you're always so happy. It's unnatural." He just grins at her. "I heard your Pa's a drunk and your mom's got to work two jobs to feed you all. Can't see that being a good time."

I watch Tattoo Girl try to smother Free Throw's joy with her darkness and wonder how deep her sources run. But Free Throw isn't flustered. "We do okay. Together as a family, we're strong." He flexes a skinny right arm and flashes a bright smile.

"Seriously. It's not like you can be happy all the time, nobody can," Tattoo Girl persists. "How come you don't get bitter and cynical like your druggie brother?"

I cringe. She's hit low and I can see it momentarily in Free Throw's eyes.

"You know Billy?" he asks, but Tattoo Girl doesn't respond. He rubs the side of his neck, then punches his hands into his pockets. "Billy's lost his way, but he'll find it back. The Lord won't abandon him."

Tattoo Girl opens her mouth then closes it again when I shoot her a scathing glance. She slaps the paint onto the wall, rolls it ferociously, then leaves to get a new can.

I watch Free Throw. Does he really believe the Lord is looking after his family, even with all their problems? "Is your whole family religious, Free Throw?"

He nods. "Catholic. What about yours?"

I contemplate for a moment. "Uh, not really . . . I mean I guess we're Christian, but we don't go to church or anything like that."

"You'd like our church," he tells me. "The music and the incense and all the girls in their strapless dresses." A sunny smile crosses his face.

"Is that why you go?"

He half-turns away from me. "Partly," he admits, and I am surprised by how guilt-laden his voice is. "But I go to confession too," he adds, looking at me sheepishly.

"With a priest?" I ask raising my eyebrows. "You tell him about the girls?"

Free Throw shifts uncomfortably until I laugh aloud. "I wouldn't," I say. His jaw relaxes and he beams at me with gratitude. "So, you go to church every Sunday?" I continue.

"Pretty much. Our priest believes in the commandments and that's the fourth one. It's how Jesus wants us to live."

I notice he hasn't said that he believes in them and dig a little deeper. "You believe in all those miracles Jesus performed too?"

"That's what the Bible says, so yeah, why not?" Free Throw looks perplexed for a moment. "You don't?"

I dip my brush into my paint can again. "Uh, I-I guess I'm not sure what to believe. I mean it seems a little farfetched, but then again it was before my time, right?"

A crease forms on Free Throw's forehead. Damn! Now I'm messing up some guy's faith. I clear my throat and quickly change the subject. "You got a thing for animals, hey Free Throw?"

A huge smile lights up his face. "Critters," he says. "My mom, she says I got more love for God's creatures and nature than I do for her."

"Well, we sure do live in a beautiful place," I say, trying to make amends for my earlier comments. It's true, I think, glancing out the window at the leaves rustling in streaks of sunlight. Just then a monarch butterfly alights on the windowsill, as if to prove my point. Free Throw holds his breath and we both watch the exquisite creature until it flits away. "It must be nice to find comfort in faith," I say, the thought still clinging to me.

Free Throw doesn't respond right away. "Yes," he says more slowly than I expect him to, "and no."

"Huh? What's that mean?"

He cracks his knuckles and his voice drops. "It's just that, you know, God wants us to be good, and we should be but, well, when we sin, there's so much guilt, you know."

I nod. He has no idea how well I know.

"And, well, I'm no Jesus, Grady, so sometimes there's a lot of guilt."

"Can't you just ask for forgiveness?" For a split second, I am aware of how ironic this conversation is. Me trying to comfort Free Throw with the idea of God and forgiveness. I'd like to believe that God is a comfort, that He took my dad home, just like Mom assured me when he died. And that I'll see him again in heaven — the only thing is, even if that's all true, I'm not sure I'll get there. I mean, how do you ask someone for forgiveness when they aren't here anymore? And isn't that a prerequisite to get through the pearly gates?

"I suppose," says Free Throw. "But even if someone forgives you, how do you know if God really forgives you for all your sins?"

Tattoo Girl has returned with another can of paint. "You change your god!" she announces as she opens the can.

"But God is God," says Free Throw, and I'm pretty sure that in his mind Tattoo Girl has just committed blasphemy.

"Yep, but which god are you talking about?" She stirs the paint, bringing dark streaks to the surface.

"The Christian God," Free Throw says tentatively.

"Which one?" she asks as she outlines on the wall with the narrow edge of her brush — a panther ready to pounce.

Free Throw is speechless, and I find myself wondering where this is going. Somehow, I hadn't expected any Christian conversation from Tattoo Girl.

"The God of the Old Testament would strike us down, instill fear in our hearts and send us all to hell for our sins," she says while adding drops of blood to the panther's fangs. "But take Jesus in the New Testament. He was all about love and forgiveness, right?" She obviously knows something about the Bible. "So, which one do you believe in?" she asks, painting the panther's tail. "The vengeful God or the loving Jesus?"

I glance at Free Throw who really doesn't know what to say, but before he can decide, Tattoo Girl adds, "If you're ignorant enough to believe in either of them."

Our minds run like the paint on her brush, but neither of us responds. Instead, we watch her paint. It is obvious that the girl has talent, and both Free Throw and I admire her art before she obliterates it with the roller, and we go back to painting in silence.

Finally, Free Throw wipes his hands on a rag. "If I could be any creature, I'd be an eagle," he says. "What a view they must have." I can almost picture him soaring high above the earth. "Then I could fly away whenever I wanted. And you?" he asks me.

I think for a minute. "A dolphin," I say, loving the intelligence and freedom of that animal. We both look at Tattoo Girl.

"Sea snake," she says, "the most lethal creature in the world."

In no time it is obvious that Free Throw's animal empathy is well beyond my understanding, despite my own affinity for four-legged creatures. By the end of the week, he has the chipmunk that resides beneath the giant poplar eating out of his hand, can perfectly whistle the robin's songs and has Walter wrapped around his long bony fingers. His shirt is always covered in ladybugs and butterflies, which bring a genuine look of wonder to his dark eyes. He even thanks the flowers for their beautiful blossoms as he deadheads them. I have given up commenting. Reg notices and tells Free Throw to check out the rabbit's burrow at the back of the community centre. Within days, the rabbits are following him through the gardens, and he's given them all saints' names.

The gardens don't end at the community centre. At the far end of the field sits that wooden house with gabled windows surrounded by a tall hedge, rose bushes and huge flower gardens. These too are our responsibility. Tattoo Girl protests the first time Reg walks us over there. "This doesn't belong to the centre. It's some rich lady's house. I've seen her."

"Me too," I add, feeling the ache in my arms and back.

"You're right," Reg says calmly, "the house doesn't belong to the centre. The centre belongs to this house." He doesn't explain. "We'll meet here tomorrow. Pick up your tools on the way over." He pauses, then adds, "And tomorrow we'll do a half-hour meditation."

Even Tattoo Girl doesn't have an answer to that.

That night Mom serves rouladen for supper. Dad's favourite. And suddenly I remember. It is Dad's birthday. Or at least it would have been. Mom doesn't say anything and neither do I. Charlotte is too young to remember and Mom doesn't want to upset her, so the menu choice is just our horrible little secret. Mom tries hard to make it special, but it's tough when the guest of honour is dead. By the time she serves the cheesecake, I can't handle it anymore. "Stop!" I say. "It's just making things worse."

Charlotte's mouth is covered in crumbs and cake. She stops chewing as tears well up in Mom's eyes. I scrape my chair back, but Mom restrains me with a hand on my arm. "You're right, Grady." She erupts into tears. "I'm sorry. I just miss him so much and I don't want you to forget him."

I know that I should stand and comfort her. Tell her that he's in a better place and that he's the hero he is. But I don't. Instead, I leave Charlotte to dab Mom's face with her strawberry-stained napkin as I hit the road with my skateboard. I'm grounded so I don't go far, just up and down the street a few times in the evening sun. But as the wheels roll along so does my memory — to that day five and a half years ago.

"Why," I whine as Dad enters the room, "do you have to work Christmas Eve?" I am in my pajamas kneeling in front of the blinking lights on the tree. Shiny bows and bags surround me, and my curiosity is insatiable. I pick up a long parcel and shake it. Normally we open one gift on Christmas Eve, before Santa's arrival, but not this year. Will says Santa's a fraud and that most kids have that figured out by age ten, but I still want to believe, so I do.

"I'll be back at seven twenty tomorrow morning and then you can open everything," Dad says.

I sulk. Dad's a firefighter and that means shift work. Normally I don't mind so much, but it sucks on holidays. "You'll probably just sit at the station doing nothing all night," I pout.

"I hope so," says Mom, smiling.

Dad pulls on his gloves. "And nobody gets to read *The Night Before Christmas* while I'm away," he warns us. "That's my job."

I hate the fact that he thinks it's funny. As Dad opens the door to depart, I yell, "Yeah, well I hope there's a fire tonight." Mom's eyes widen and Dad turns towards me. "And I hope you go in and don't come out!" Mom gasps, but Dad just grins, raises his hand and waves. I slam the front door, then stomp upstairs to my bedroom. Mom puts Charlotte to bed and settles in for a bedtime story, but I refuse to join them. I imagine Dad sitting in the station kitchen, drinking coffee and reading the paper. He should be home, reading *The Night Before Christmas* after we've opened our Christmas Eve gift, as he does every year. When Mom comes in to say goodnight, I pretend to be asleep and soon I am.

The fire is only five blocks away, but I don't even hear the sirens.

# CHAPTER 4

There are four of us the next day. A tallish blond girl wearing generic jeans and a hot pink T-shirt is standing beside Reg when we arrive at the fancy house, shovels and hoes in hand. "Everyone, this is Nikki," Reg says. "Nikki, this is Margaret —"

"Tattoo Girl," comes the immediate correction.

"Grady and Free Throw," adds Reg.

"Greetings," says Nikki. Her ice-blue eyes flit constantly back and forth, her energy moving like electrons ricocheting and bounding.

"What're you here for?" asks Tattoo Girl. I wince and wonder if she gives out what she gets.

Nikki answers with an emotionless cadence. "I hacked into an educational institution's computer system."

We don't ask why, but my gut tells me it wasn't to upgrade her marks. Her restlessness unnerves me. It's sharp and barbed as if even the dandelion-seed parachutes could snag on its edges.

Reg gives us our assignments for the day. I grimace when he tells us that Nikki and I are to weed the garden in the backyard, while Free Throw and Tattoo Girl tend to the front. Nikki looks unaccustomed to a hoe, so I start, pulling up quack grass and chickweed as I work. She watches me, then looks down at her own cultivator and comments. "That is a very inefficient implement. If the two prongs were curved slightly, it would function far more effectively." She lets it fall to the ground.

"It works okay," I say pointedly, "when you're actually holding it."

"Is your name short for O'Grady?" she asks. "Your fair hair and skin suggest an Irish heritage."

"Nope, just Grady. And yours?"

"I am named after Nikola Tesla."

"Who?"

"Nikola Tesla — perhaps the greatest inventor of the twentieth century. You likely know him for alternating current or AC, which is what most of our electrical appliances now run on."

"I see." I wait, knowing she'll go on.

"Nikola Tesla demonstrated unique thought processes from an early age. My parents, being scientists themselves, hoped that I would emulate my namesake and go on to be a brilliant inventor."

"And?"

"I am not Tesla's equal," replies Nikki matter-of-factly.

"How do you know?" I protest.

"I have had no brilliant idea to date."

"How old are you?"

"Fourteen."

I pull the quack grass roots free. "Well, hacking into the school's computer system is pretty clever. Which school do you go to?"

"I attend university."

My cultivator stops mid-air. "So, you're a genius then."

"I wouldn't use that term," she replies. Picking up a shovel, she makes a feeble attempt to dig without breaking the surface of the soil. I stare at her stick-like arms and sigh. This is going to be a long day.

By lunch, I am thoroughly convinced that Nikki lives in her own world, and it is one I will never enter. I'm good with that, but it is also a world where weeds will overrun flowers if she is left to tend them. I think about asking Reg if we can switch partners. I'd rather have Free Throw's upbeat honesty, but I know that Tattoo Girl would likely kill Nikki, so I don't. Besides, lunch is a surprise.

At exactly noon, Reg invites us into a small gazebo where the table is set for six with woven placemats and cut flowers. "Mrs. Stafford has invited you all for lunch," he tells us. "There's a sink in the utility room just through the walk-out door there. Go wash up. I'll fetch Walter."

I go first and return to find a woman, maybe sixty or so judging by the wisps of grey in her hair, placing trays of fancy wraps with sprouts and avocado on the table. "Well, hello, you must be Grady." Her voice is melodic and welcoming.

I nod confirmation. "It is very kind of you to make us lunch."

"I always like to meet Reg's kids," she says. A small bichon-Shih Tzu darts out of the open screen door in my direction. "Oh, we can't forget Penny."

But Penny has already made a 180-degree turn and is headed towards Free Throw. He scoops her up and gets an enthusiastic licking from the little dog.

"And you are Free Throw! I'm Teresa Stafford and that is Penny. Reg told me she'd take a liking to you."

A robin whistles above us and the little cream and apricot-coloured dog barks happily. "My husband used to whistle all the time," says Mrs. Stafford. "She adored him and whenever he whistled, she'd reply." Free Throw whistles a bird song and she erupts into a barking fit again.

**THE NOTHING CLUB**

The girls arrive together, a study in contrasts. Mrs. Stafford introduces herself and Reg arrives with Walter. We sit to eat, and the wraps are delicious. There are also plenty, enough to fill Free Throw, who eats six at Mrs. Stafford's urging.

"The community centre property was donated by Mrs. Stafford," Reg informs us. "Her father originally owned a large farm here, but when the city annexed it, he sold some, and later Mrs. Stafford donated this parcel for the pool and centre."

"Well, back then it was a dance hall mostly, but over the years it's been added to and renovated." Mrs. Stafford pauses. "My late husband and I moved up here from the States when my father died. Now it's just me and Penny and Walter."

"And that," says Reg, eyeing Tattoo Girl and me, "is why we maintain the house property as well."

Mrs. Stafford asks about our families. We already know Free Throw's family history, and I'm not surprised to learn that Nikki is an only child. Mrs. Stafford turns her attention to Tattoo Girl. "Are you an only child also?"

Tattoo Girl lowers her eyes and tugs at the collar of her jean jacket. "Sort of," she replies, then adds, "but technically, there are two of me."

"Identical twins," explains Nikki, while I struggle with Tattoo Girl's meaning. "What's your sister's name?"

"Elizabeth," comes the soft reply. "Beth." Tattoo Girl straightens up in her chair. "Grady's turn," she says and that is that.

Lunch is followed by homemade chocolate chip cookies and slices of watermelon. Mrs. Stafford sits in the gazebo beaming at us, ensuring that we all eat more than we can stomach. Near the end of the meal, Tattoo Girl suddenly rises with alarm in her eyes. She is staring at Mrs. Stafford, who appears dazed. The woman's arms move rather haphazardly, and she sways in her chair.

Reg leans across the table. "Did you eat anything?" he asks her, lines of concern on his forehead. "Or did you just feed all these kids and not bother to eat yourself?" There is a look of gentle admonishment in his eyes.

"Very well," Mrs. Stafford says. "I will go test."

In response to our confused looks, she explains, "I have diabetes. I suspect I'm a little low, but my testing kit is inside. You kids stay and finish up the cookies."

She staggers a little as she pushes her chair back, and Reg jumps up to accompany her to the house. "I'll take you inside. The kids can clean up."

We watch them until they disappear through the walk-out door.

"Diabetes — a disease of the pancreas where the body is unable to produce sufficient insulin and, therefore, control its blood sugars," Nikki explains.

"She looks drunk," says Free Throw.

"A state caused by insufficient blood sugars," says Nikki. "Her testing kit will likely indicate that to be the case; she will then rectify this either by ingesting something sweet or taking a glucose tablet. By contrast, if her blood sugars get too high, she will inject herself with insulin to maintain a desirable level."

"You mean she shoots up with insulin?" asks Free Throw.

"Something like that," I say, "on a regular basis." My cousin has diabetes. I am reminded of the time we went to a movie, and he appeared to fall asleep in the seat beside me. I elbowed him and when he didn't respond, I whispered to his sister that he was missing a great show. We all missed it in the end when we went to the hospital.

"So, what happens if her sugars get really, really low?" asks Free Throw.

"She will suffer a diabetic coma and die."

"Super," drawls Tattoo Girl.

"Given her slim figure and healthy diet, I would guess that Mrs. Stafford is Type 1, meaning that she was likely born with this medical condition. Most people with Type 1 diabetes are diagnosed by age ten or eleven, but even small babies can suffer from the condition."

"Can't they do something to cure it?" asks Free Throw.

"Diabetic research is very advanced. One of the best hopes for diabetes now is to reprogram stem cells."

"Which are?" I ask. "I mean I've heard of them but —"

"Which are the master cells in the body. They can produce both more cells like themselves and other types of cells through a process called differentiation. In persons with diabetes, their insulin-producing cells no longer function normally, so what scientists are attempting to do is to turn stem cells into differentiated insulin-producing cells." She pauses, in awe. "It's radical and yet so simple. If they can reprogram those cells to be like they would be in an embryo, then implant them, they should turn into normal pancreatic cells."

"Wow!" I say. "That would cure someone like Mrs. Stafford forever!" And my cousin, I think. "That's quite the accomplishment."

"Yes," agrees Nikki. "And medical researchers believe the whole cure could take less than three months." She emits a heavy sigh. "It may well be Nobel Peace Prize worthy. And if it works and can be applied to other bodily malfunctions, well it would revolutionize medicine." She looks at us and her expression is one of discomfort and disappointment.

"Wouldn't that be a good thing?" I ask.

Nikki snaps upright. "An excellent thing," she says, "although it would set the bar for future accomplishments very high."

"You're only fourteen and already in university," I remind her. I am grateful that my extraordinarily ordinary abilities mean that life is without such expectations.

Reg returns and we gather up the dishes and march up the deck stairs, through a patio door into a bright family room with expensive leather couches and antique lamps. I slip my shoes off at the door and the others do the same. Framed photos cover one wall — children of all ages. I wonder how many grandchildren Mrs. Stafford has and why she didn't mention them. A portrait hangs over the fireplace — a young Mrs. Stafford, her husband and a small blond girl about Charlotte's age. A family portrait. I look again at the photos in the gallery. All are of the little blond girl at various ages throughout her life.

Tattoo Girl hollers at me to get into the kitchen and help, so I carry the plates in. It is a beautiful room with rich cherrywood cabinets and spotless granite countertops. Mrs. Stafford returns and directs us, and in no time the kitchen is pristine. When we are done, Tattoo Girl asks to use the washroom and Reg points down the hall. "Mrs. Stafford is a wonderful woman," he tells her, "with a great respect for personal belongings."

"I'm just going pee," she fires back. He grins at her and lingers in the kitchen while the rest of us wait outside with our hostess.

"Do you have children?" I ask Mrs. Stafford.

She purses her lips momentarily. "We had a daughter, Adrianna. But she died at the age of eight from complications related to diabetes."

"I'm so sorry," I murmur.

Beside me, Free Throw sways awkwardly. "My mom always says God works in mysterious ways, but taking the life of a child . . ." There is an uncharacteristic gravity in his voice, and his long fingers tap his chest, above his heart. The guy feels deeply, of that I am sure.

Reg and Tattoo Girl emerge from the house, and we thank Mrs. Stafford for a delicious lunch. She takes her leave, explaining that she has an appointment in half an hour. Her blood sugars seem fine now.

And then Reg announces that it is time for meditation.

"You're serious," complains Tattoo Girl. "Is this even legal?"

"According to my research, engaging in meditation breaks no laws," replies Nikki, who doesn't understand a rhetorical question. "It is intended to shift the brain waves — synchronized electrical pulses — from our daily alpha waves to theta waves, which are associated with creativity, increased problem-solving skills and calmness."

"Say what?" asks Free Throw.

"In short, meditation is intended to decrease anxiety and stress and boost problem-solving abilities and emotional stability. It appears to alter your brain waves, which in turn augments — uh, increases — your positive energy, whatever that is."

"You meditate?" asks Free Throw.

"Negative," replies Nikki. "But I researched it and discovered that positive energy has an entirely different meaning in physics than it does in psychology." Her voice drips with skepticism.

Reg intervenes. "Positive energy," he says, "is energy that's not negative."

Nikki bristles. "Defining something in terms of what it is not may be possible, but it is not sufficient."

"Well then," says Reg, pulling a small speaker off a shelf in the shed, "think of it this way. Positive energy brings positive thoughts, which in turn manifest positive experiences."

Tattoo Girl lets out a low whistle. "The famous law of attraction."

There is a coolness to her words that disturbs me, and I wonder why, if it's so famous, I've never heard of it. "So if it's linked to the *law* of attraction, meditation really is legal then," I quip, trying to lighten the moment. Nobody laughs.

"What do we do, Reg?" asks Free Throw, jumping in before Nikki can offer any further unscientific commentary.

Reg hands us each a yoga mat. "Pull up a comfortable piece of lawn, lie down on your back and focus on your breathing. In for four counts and out for eight. In and out. Just let your mind go quiet. Don't think of anything. If you do, just let the thought go and then return to that stillness." He unrolls his mat, then pairs his cell phone to the speaker.

"And what exactly are we hoping to experience?" asks Nikki.

"We'll see," is all Reg says.

Free Throw exuberantly spreads his yoga mat, kicks off his shoes and flops down, while Nikki and I hesitantly follow suit.

We watch Tattoo Girl, who waits, muscles tense, and I wonder if she's going to toss the yoga mat and bolt. Finally, she unrolls the mat and sits on it. Reg starts the meditation recording.

I squint into the sun, then close my eyes as two chimes ring. A serene male voice instructs us.

*Lying flat on your back on a bed or a mat in a comfortable place where you are unlikely to be disturbed, focus on your breath. Inhale, then exhale. Inhale to the count of four and exhale to the count of eight. In and out. Focusing only on your breath.*

I breathe deeply, counting silently and focusing on my breath. I wonder what the squirrels must think of us.

*If your mind wanders, simply bring your attention back to your breath. In and out, in and out. Breathe deeply. Inhale. Exhale. Breathe.*

I bring my thoughts back to my breath, then immediately feel a gust of wind. Again, I reorient myself. The voice drones on. Suddenly chimes ring again and I hear Reg rise.

I open my eyes, sit up and glance at Tattoo Girl, half-expecting to see her penetrating stare judging me, but she is still prone, her mascara-blackened eyes blinking open. For the first time, I notice how grey they are. Pewter like. Quite beautiful and unique. Nikki is on her knees and Free Throw is already on his feet, rolling up his mat.

I do the same, wondering if I nodded off or where my mind went. I don't have much recollection of the time that must have passed. I store my mat, waiting for Reg to expound on the virtues of meditation or ask us to recount our meditative experiences, but true to his nature, he does neither. Instead, he tells us that we will be switching partners for the afternoon, and I will work with Tattoo Girl.

Rain threatens and we weed in silence. The meditation has left me quieter on the inside. It makes me slow and measured. But that is not the case for Tattoo Girl. Rather, she moves in an almost frenzied, irritable manner. I watch her disturb the ground, pulling chickweed with her tattooed hands and wonder if her parents are tattooed as well or how she ever got permission to decorate her body like that at her age. Then again, she doesn't seem like the type to ask for permission. The yard is fenced on three sides with a tall hedge on the fourth, and Tattoo Girl moves to the hedge while I work on one of the long flower beds alongside the house. "I'm going to fill my water bottle from the hose," I call to her, but she is gone.

Dropping my shovel, I wander towards the hedge. Her pitchfork lies on the ground, but there is not a patch of her ink-stained skin visible. Squatting down, I peer through a hole in the branches. She is standing on the sidewalk talking to a guy with a shaved head. He wears a leather vest over his bare chest, frayed jeans and both his arms are covered in full tattoo sleeves. Tattoo Girl shakes her head, and I can't shake the feeling that this guy is bad news. For a moment, I think I ought to step out of hiding and call to her, loud enough for Reg, who is working in the garage, to hear.

Tattoo Girl turns, but the bald guy grabs her wrist and holds her. She struggles and he drops her arm. I can tell by her body language that she is upset, but he puts two hands on her shoulders, and she stays put. Again, she shakes her head. Again, my lips form her name, but I remain mute. The guy leans towards her and whispers something. I see her nod and then I see Reg.

He moves pretty well for a middle-aged guy — half-sprinting across the lawn, a shovel over his shoulder. Bald Guy takes a step back. Tattoo Girl looks alarmed. Her long, straight hair sweeps one way then the other. Reg has reached them. He holds the shovel in one arm and points with his other hand. "This is private property and you're trespassing," he says. I am unnerved by the quiet authority of his voice.

Bald Guy shrugs. "So what, man!" he protests. "It's a free world."

I can't hear what Reg says next because he lowers his voice, but soon Bald Guy takes another step backwards onto the sidewalk. Tattoo Girl tries to intervene, but Reg raises one open hand, and she stops. He leans towards Bald Guy. "Now please leave the property and do not return." His voice is serene and patient, like he is talking to Walter. He rests the spade on the ground.

Bald Guy retreats onto the street. He points in Tattoo Girl's direction, but she has turned away from him. "Oh," calls Reg, "if you hurry you can watch your buddy in the black pickup truck get questioned by the cops."

Tattoo Girl freaks. "Rigoh's here?" she screams. "You never said anything about Rigoh." She clenches her fist and bellows, "What the hell are you trying to do to me?" She lunges towards him, but Reg blocks her way and Bald Guy bolts. Tattoo Girl screams after him, "You promised me, man. You promised. And then you brought him here." She is shaking in fury.

Reg puts one hand on her shoulder and grounds her. "Breathe," he instructs her, "just breathe."

Nikki and Free Throw have joined me now, and we all peer through the hedge. Reg slides his back down a nearby tree trunk and motions for Tattoo Girl to join him. She does, sinking onto the grass, then resting her head on her knees. We can't hear their conversation but even so, I somehow feel as if we are invading a private moment. "Guess we better get back to work," I say and the others nod. A rabbit sits beside Free Throw, and he reaches down and strokes its ears. I don't even think it's odd. After what just happened, nothing seems odd.

Tattoo Girl doesn't say anything when she returns. I watch her but her eyes are clouded over, and she is lost in a dark fog somewhere. Reg lets us all go early. She doesn't say goodbye.

## CHAPTER 5

On the weekend, I'm lounging in the family room when Charlotte races in with a shiny quarter. "Will you teach me how to do a coin trick?" she asks. "Alice's brother can make one disappear." I grimace at her words. Coin tricks were Dad's thing. I can almost see my father reaching to pull a coin out of my right ear as he tucks me into bed. "Nope," I tell Charlotte whose bottom lip pushes itself into a pout. "No, I will not." She pockets the coin with a sigh and traipses outside.

A quiet sadness seeps through me punctuated by the usual pang of guilt just as Mom enters the room. I notice she doesn't have a phone stuck to her ear. She settles on the couch opposite me and asks how I'm doing in community service. "Tell me about the others," she invites.

I shrug. I'm not sure why she wants to know about the days I spend with a bunch of kids with nothing in common except that we all screwed up in life. But she seems genuinely interested, so I tell her briefly about the four of us, and what we got community service for, except for Tattoo Girl because I don't know. I leave out the part about Rigoh. There are some things it's better that she doesn't know.

"And what's Reg like?"

"Quiet, wise and foreboding when he has to be."

She raises one eyebrow at me, and I admit that that's not the answer she probably expected. Nevertheless, it's true. She adjusts herself in her seat and chews on her bottom lip momentarily. "Uh, Grady, there's an open house at Fire Station 57 this weekend," she begins. "Charlotte and I are going — you know how she loves fire trucks — and I wondered if you —"

"No!" I tell her, leaping to my feet. "Count me out!" I storm out the patio door wondering when she's ever going to stop.

After Dad died, I read all those near-death experience accounts and dozens of testimonies about departed souls watching over their loved ones on Earth. Every night for a month, I prayed that Dad would come back. Then I downgraded my request to a mere visit — a request for a short conversation so I could take back my parting words. After six months, it was obvious that either he wasn't going to show or God wasn't going to help me, or both.

I wonder if Nikki ever asks anyone for help but somehow, I doubt it. She's the one I can't figure out. I mean she's obviously a genius since she's at university already, and yet she thinks she's a real loser. Maybe it's because she has such high-achieving parents. Her dad's a biomedical engineer and inventor, and her mom's some world-renowned cancer researcher. It's no wonder she thinks she's got to be a Nikola Tesla or someone.

One day at lunch, Tattoo Girl and I find her with her eyes closed and her hands perfectly still by her side. Her energy is so intense that I find myself staring at her without apology. I'm amazed that anyone can think that hard.

Tattoo Girl slumps down against the shed, watching me watch Nikki. Nikki's stomach rumbles and we both laugh. Her eyes snap open. "Have you eaten anything?" I ask. "You sound hungry."

She stomps a foot. "There are more important things to do than eat, Grady. I am trying to solve a problem that has perplexed me for some weeks now."

Tattoo Girl and I dig into our lunches. I pull out an apple just as Tattoo Girl does the same. "I have an apple if you want," she offers.

"Me too," I chime in without looking up. "It's a Gala," we both say in unison, then lock eyes and laugh.

I feel Nikki's gaze on us before I glance towards her. She looks horrified. "What did you say?"

"That you can have my —" Tattoo Girl begins.

But Nikki cuts her off. "Did you both just offer me a Gala apple?"

"Uh, yeah, but, I mean, if you don't like them, then, hey . . ." I say.

"Why?" asks Nikki, wide-eyed. "Why did you both offer me that particular type of apple at that precise moment?"

I gesture palms up and Tattoo Girl rolls her eyes. "Let's see. Maybe because we both have one and because your stomach was growling," she says in a voice that bites. "What have you got up your ass?"

Nikki's fingers splay. "I was, at that exact moment, contemplating the specific modifications to my apple corer, peeler and slicer implement needed to accommodate a Red Gala apple. You both offering me a Gala apple, by name, at the precise moment of my contemplation is . . . is, well, uncanny." Then she adds, "And statistically highly improbable. So, explain please."

I can't so I don't.

Nikki gets to her feet. "My thoughts are not transparent." She approaches me and despite all of her forty-five kilos, she is rather menacing. "I didn't say a word. I never do when I'm imaging and I have told no one about this invention. Explain, Grady! Margaret!"

Tattoo Girl scowls, then makes a show of biting into her Gala apple, while the juices run down her lip. She stays pointedly silent.

Nikki leans towards me.

"I-I don't know," I stammer.

Nikki stares incredulously at me. "Can you read my mind?"

"I cannot nor do I understand most of what's in your mind," I tell her. And even she knows that's the honest truth.

Tattoo Girl feigns a yawn. "It was just coincidence. Right?" I ask her. She can at least help me out a little here.

She chews thoughtfully. "I suppose, although sometimes people — like me and Grady — can tune in to what other people are thinking."

Nikki slaps her outstretched hands on her legs. "So, you don't read minds, but you know what others are thinking? What's the difference?"

"It is different," insists Tattoo Girl. "Sometimes I just know stuff; everyone does."

"Yeah," I agree. Nikki glares at me expectantly, and against my better judgement, I continue. "It's just . . . well, I mean, it's like how you just pick up vibes sometimes?"

"Vibes?" She is growing exasperated. "So, what do you do, visualize vibrating air molecules and arrange them in multiple permutations and combinations until you ascertain the frequency of the one that is most statistically possible given the situational context?"

Tattoo Girl snorts.

"Wow! I wish," I say. "Actually, I think it's a lot less scientific and a lot more . . ." I search for the word. "Weird." I have to admit that it was a pretty strange moment, but Tattoo Girl's right; those bizarre things just happen from time to time. Most people just don't have to analyze them like Nikki has to.

"Extrapolate!" she demands, relentlessly dragging me back to the question at hand.

"Uh, weird as in coincidental, strange, kind of . . ." I stumble through my thoughts as Nikki crosses her arms and taps her foot impatiently. "Kind of out there."

"Out there where? In which domain? Ethereal, metaphysical, spiritual?"

"Uh, maybe spiritual," I say, since it's the only word I recognize.

"Spiritual? Pertaining to the human soul or spirit as opposed to something physical or material that can be understood with our senses. That kind of spiritual?"

"I'm, uh, not sure." I mean, I've never really thought about it like that. I glance at the sun as if I can discern time from its position in the sky. "Uh, we gotta get back to work," I say, even though I know it's still early.

Tattoo Girl rises to her feet and dusts off her jeans. She chucks her apple core in the compost pile, then saunters off in silence. I follow, knowing that Nikki's mind is racing after us.

The next morning, Nikki shows up with a steel box. Encased within it is a small metal headband with wires hanging off it. She removes it gingerly from its fabric lining.

"What is that?" I ask.

"One of my father's inventions. It's basically a wearable electroencephalographic device designed to measure and classify brain waves." The blank look in my eyes spurs her on to a simpler explanation. "You wear it, and I look at the data on my phone to see which areas of your brain are working . . . if any." I grin at the slight. It's so not Nikki. But she is all business again in the next breath. "So . . . lunchtime, Grady, be here!"

I don't have a choice, but Free Throw and Tattoo Girl do, so why they opt to come along is beyond me.

"First," explains Nikki as we gather around, "I need to understand the components of this *spiritual* energy you all seem to know about." She gestures with her hands in which she holds the metal headband. "Sit, Grady!" she instructs. "I confess that I know little about the spiritual domain and could find virtually nothing scholarly or scientific by way of research last night," she adds as I perch on the bench in front of her, removing my baseball cap and running fingers through my sweaty hair.

"No kidding." Tattoo Girl laughs.

"What does that mean?" Nikki questions her in earnest but gets no response. She redirects her attention to Free Throw. "How about you? Do you understand such spiritual concepts?"

"Well, I guess prayer is like that," replies Free Throw. "God hears us and answers our prayers, but we can't really explain how."

I would disagree based on my personal experience but say nothing, unwilling to challenge Free Throw's convictions again. The headband has now been placed on my scalp and adjusted so that it is snug. Wires dangle down both cheeks and my forehead.

"So, you think that spirituality is religion?" asks Nikki.

"No!" Tattoo Girl's response is too adamant.

"Well, I suppose it can be an aspect of religion," I say glancing at Free Throw.

"Does that mean you believe in God, Grady?"

"Uh, well, I, uh, I don't really know what I believe in," I reply. Nikki opens a package of wet wipes and cleans the skin on my forehead and behind my ears.

"And you don't?" Nikki asks turning to Tattoo Girl.

Tattoo Girl doesn't hesitate. "Correct!"

Free Throw shifts his weight from one foot to the other. "You know the Bible so well," he says, addressing Tattoo Girl. "But you don't believe in God?"

"I used to because I grew up in the Christian religion," she says sweetly, "but then I started to think for myself."

Ouch! I try to soften the blow for Free Throw. "What's religion anyway?" I ask to ease the tension. "Isn't it —"

"Dogma relating to a system of external beliefs associated with a theological institution," interrupts Nikki.

Technically she's right, but that wasn't my point. Nikki removes a pack of electrodes from a plastic pouch and inserts short wires into them. Finally, she connects the lead wires from the metal headband to the electrode wires.

"Is this going to hurt?" I ask touching the headband tentatively.

Nikki ignores my question. Instead, she studies the others with an expression of curiosity and insight. "So," she summarizes, "Free Throw's a believer, Grady's an agnostic and Tattoo Girl's an atheist. But you all seem to understand events in the spiritual domain, which, by definition, suggest that there is more to life than that which we can experience on a physical level." She pauses as we all try to digest her words. "I do not comprehend."

Tattoo Girl clenches her jaw. "Okay, you know, that déjà vu feeling you get sometimes?"

Nikki shakes her head.

"Oh, come on, everyone has that experience at one time or another."

Nikki stands taller. "Apparently I deviate from everyone's experiences," she concedes, and I'm pretty sure she's right.

Tattoo Girl bristles. "It's a feeling you have when something's happening — like you've already lived through that experience."

"Impossible," Nikki informs her. "We live for an average of seventy-nine years on this earth, and time moves in a single direction only on this earthly plane."

"You're sure stupid for a genius." Tattoo Girl throws up her hands in exasperation, but Nikki does not seem to be insulted.

I try to mediate. "Well, there may not be a scientific explanation for everything that happens, uh, sometimes."

Nikki begins to pace. She appears to have completely forgotten that I am seated in front of her with some brainwave measuring device flattening my hair and electrodes protruding from the contraption.

Tattoo Girl spins on the heel of her boot. "Okay, once I was standing watch while this deal went down and I just had this feeling that I'd done it before. That time the cops came busting through this white gate, and sure enough there's this white gate just next to me, so I sounded the alarm, and we beat it out of there just before the sirens came." She pauses and I wonder if she's meant to reveal what she has. "Only Rigoh was pissed, really pissed 'cause he was close to a big deal."

The silence that follows is barbed. I jump in before Nikki can interrogate Tattoo Girl further. "Or when you know something's going to happen because you dream it or see it and then months, even years later, you're living it."

"Like?" prompts Nikki.

"Like I used to have this dream about my dad, and it came true one day." Six eyes stare expectantly at me. "I used to dream about his death . . . and it happened that way." Nobody asks but the pressure builds. I don't want to tell. Free Throw saves me.

"Once when my older brother got knifed . . ." He glances up at Tattoo Girl.

She meets his eyes without judgement. "Go on," she says softly.

"In my left quad, I felt this awful pain. So, I prayed, and God helped me figure out where Billy was, so I could find him and get help."

"So, spirituality is about synchronicities, intuition and in some cases, messages from the divine?" paraphrases Nikki.

"Sure," I say.

Nikki's demeanour softens. I watch her carefully as her pacing ceases and her composure returns. "Once my dad left an article on a recent genetic manipulation on the table. I read it, and the long answer exam question in my genetics course was on that exact manipulation." She smirks. "The prof was so impressed that I'd figured it out on my own, and I never told him otherwise."

Our energy envelops her as her phone alarm announces the end of lunch; she removes the metal headband and replaces it in its case.

## CHAPTER 6

That afternoon we have our daily meditation again. The strange thing is that I find myself looking forward to it. Even Tattoo Girl has unrolled her yoga mat before Reg arrives. What is it, I wonder, about being still?

But as soon as Reg arrives, Nikki has begun analyzing the unanalyzable. "I have spent hours contemplating the manner in which we might know things that it is not logically possible to know," she begins as I roll my eyes. She can be annoyingly relentless. "I believe others explain such events in terms of getting vibes, or déjà vu or even prayer, which seems somewhat casually related to spirituality, which appears to be anecdotally related to this process of meditation in which we might be expected to gain insights into ourselves or our lives that are not available to us in a rational state." She takes a deep breath.

"Uh-huh," says Reg scrolling through his cell phone.

"So, how does that happen?" Nikki's voice rises an octave, and I see Reg swallow a smile.

"Have you ever heard of a dog whistle?" he asks her.

I purse my lips as Nikki's impatience flares. "High-pitched whistles outside the scope of human hearing but within the range of a canine's, generally used to recall a dog upon command."

"Well, like you said, we can't hear it, right?"

"Correct."

"But that doesn't mean it doesn't exist. In fact, the dog's response, amongst other things, indicates the whistle actually makes a sound," says Reg slowly. I think I know where he's going with this. "Vibrations, prayer, premonitions, these other so-called spiritual events, well they're kind of the same. Things happen that we can't explain or understand with our five senses, but that doesn't mean that they don't exist or that they aren't real."

"Just that they are outside of our ability to register," concludes Nikki.

"Yes, you can either dismiss such events as nonsensical or you can explore them from a different frame of reference."

"Such as?" asks Nikki.

"Such as the possibility that intuitions, hunches, miracles and other phenomena are associated with some sort of expanded consciousness." Reg clears his throat as Nikki's eyes flit furiously, indicating that the wheels in her head are beginning to spin — fast. And just like that Reg hits play, and our meditation begins.

Nikki says nothing when the meditation ends, but I sense something has altered within her. She barely seems to notice when Reg informs us that we will be helping drain and clean the pool for the next three days. And yet at the same time, she is totally focused.

Cleaning the pool is intense work because the community doesn't want it shut for long. Catherine and Scott, the lifeguard, will be giving us a hand.

Scott is a potential future candidate for *The Bachelor* reality TV show. Tanned, handsome with a six-pack, or "sex pack" as

Tattoo Girl calls it, and oozing animal magnetism. He watches us come into the pool area and gestures unhappily. "This is my team?" he asks loudly enough for us all to hear. "They're a bunch of delinquents. They know nothing. Nothing!"

Tattoo Girl steps forward, and I know the likes of Scott are enough to unleash her. I feel sorry for him for a moment, but Free Throw comes to his aid. He grabs the collar of Tattoo Girl's jean jacket, pulls her back and steps in front of her, extending a long gangly arm to Scott. "Free Throw, proud member of the Nothing Club," he says smiling broadly. And so we are named.

Scott looks at him in disgust, then reluctantly bumps the outstretched fist with his own. "I hope you know how to take orders."

Catherine slips through the concession door and joins us. "Scott knows the drill as far as the pool goes, so he's going to explain the protocol," says Reg. Noticing Catherine, Scott points a single tanned finger at her. She blushes, stumbles and blushes a deeper shade of red.

"Ooh, she's got it bad for him," whispers Tattoo Girl. "I hate when girls go for that roll-on charm."

I sense that I have none in her eyes and wonder if I should be complimented or offended.

We divide into groups and get to work, Scott barking orders over our heads, working like a Trojan himself. I work with Tattoo Girl and try to keep her distracted so she doesn't knock Scott into the pool with her brush. Not that he can't swim, but the pool is almost empty.

By the end of the morning, we are hot, sweaty and grumpy. Reg instructs Catherine to get everyone an ice cream bar and we relax in the shade, our legs stretched out before us. Scott has disappeared into an air-conditioned office to speak with his supervisor. When he returns, he is eager to continue. "How about we take a short lunch and get out of here early?"

"How about we knock you unconscious and tattoo *Asshole* on your forehead," Tattoo Girl counters.

"Half an hour," states Scott as we groan.

Tattoo Girl regards him with contempt. "I'll tell you what. If I can guess your birthday month, we take an hour. If not, we do a thirty-minute lunch."

Scott pauses, his hands on his hips. "The odds of her being able to do that are one in twelve or 8.3 percent," Nikki calculates.

Smugly, Scott crosses his arms over his bare, suntanned chest. "Okay," he says, giving her a sassy smile, "guess away."

Tattoo Girl doesn't hesitate. "April," she states decisively.

Scott's arms fall and his jaw drops open momentarily. "How did . . . someone told you. Fine," he grunts as he heads towards the concession. "But no more than an hour."

We turn to Tattoo Girl. "How did you do that?" asks Free Throw. He grins like a small child. "Can you guess mine?"

"December," comes the response from behind closed eyes.

"Wow! That's right. December eleventh. That's so cool." Free Throw gives her a thumbs up. "Do Grady's and Nikki's."

"Nikki was born in October and Grady in March."

Nikki's eyes widen and I know her birthday month is correct, but I shake my head.

Tattoo Girl opens her eyes. "Okay then, Grady was born in late February, right?"

"February twenty-seventh," I admit. "How'd you know?"

"Zodiac signs." Tattoo Girl's darkened eyelids close and nothing follows. I know that I am a Pisces in the zodiac calendar, but that doesn't explain much.

Nikki clears her throat and Tattoo Girl sighs. "Okay, okay," she says. "Depending on your date of birth, each of you is a specific zodiac sign. They don't quite correspond to months but almost. That's why I got Grady's wrong first. But he's still a Pisces. You can tell because he's sensitive, emotional and calm on the outside."

Everyone looks at me. I shrug. She's nailed me, especially with the reference to "on the outside."

"And Nikki is a Virgo — reliable, detailed and methodical, with a propensity towards perfectionism."

Nikki nods. "That would summarize my personality in an accurate manner."

Tattoo Girl tilts her head towards Free Throw. "Sagittarius. Nature and animal loving, free-spirited and annoyingly optimistic."

That does seem like Free Throw. "What's Catherine?" I ask suddenly curious.

Tattoo Girl pauses. "I'd guess she's a Taurus," she says finally. "Likely born in May."

I make a mental note to ask Catherine her birthday.

Scott marches onto the pool deck. "Aries," decrees Tattoo Girl, "arrogant, self-centred and likes to lead."

We get to our feet and reluctantly resume work. Reg doesn't suggest we meditate that day, and I find myself missing the chance to contemplate. Apparently, I'm not the only one. I'm in the middle of lifting a bench with Nikki when she suddenly stands up, sending the wooden structure crashing to the pool deck, narrowly missing my toe.

"How can birthdates reveal personality?" she asks. "Is that also a component of the spiritual realm?"

I look over my shoulder, but there's nobody else close enough to hear her. "I think that's a question for Reg," I reply, gesturing at Nikki's end of the bench and taking my feet out of harm's way. "Are you always this curious?"

Nikki ponders my question for a moment. "Of course,"

she says as Reg hustles by us carrying a large box. "Curiosity is the cornerstone of science."

"And spiritualism," interjects Reg without stopping.

Nikki's eyes glaze over with that all-too-familiar obsessive look she gets. Scott spots us doing nothing and storms in our direction. "Well, there's nothing positive or spiritual heading towards us right now, and I don't have to be psychic to know that," I tell her.

"Psychic?" she muses aloud as Scott wrenches the bench out of my hand and carries it off above his head. Nikki hardly notices.

Mid-afternoon, Reg suggests we all take a hydration break. As I relax on a piece of lawn outside the pool, I find myself wondering why Nikki doesn't just dismiss all this inexplicable stuff as non-scientific. "So, I'm confused. Do you believe in any of that spiritual stuff or not?" I ask her finally. For some reason, it seems important to know. Maybe because I've hardly thought of any of this before now.

"I am a scientist, Grady. Spiritualism, religion and faith — all those concepts — are simply not rational. The probability of anything in that realm being proven, explained or accepted by the scientific community seems unlikely."

"I disagree." Reg has come up behind us. He sinks down into the shade and rests his elbows on bent knees. "In fact, sometimes I think scientists understand spirituality better than theologians." He takes a long swig from his water bottle as Nikki fidgets impatiently. "Scientists believe in hypotheses, correct?"

"Correct. We create a hypothesis, test it and then draw conclusions from our results. That is the scientific way."

"And those experiments don't always yield conclusive results, right?"

"That also is true," acknowledges Nikki.

"In fact, in some instances, it's hard to know what is probable and what is real," observes Reg.

"Like in what instances?" I ask, my curiosity piqued.

"Like Schrödinger's cat in the box experiment," Nikki admits.

Shadows fall across the lawn, and Free Throw's voice rings out behind us as he and Tattoo Girl approach. "Who put a cat in a box?"

They settle into our patch of shade as Nikki explains. "In the first half of the twentieth century, physicists were seeking to explain things that defied scientific understanding at that time. Things like how light behaves."

Reg elucidates. "It had been scientifically proven that light acts as a wave, but it had also been shown that it acts as a particle, and scientists couldn't agree on which it was."

"The debate centred on the behaviour of subatomic particles or quanta," explains Nikki. "Basically, it examined the idea that these quanta — or photons in the case of light — can exist in two simultaneous states, and only become one or the other when detected by an observer or when an interaction with other quanta occurs."

"Huh?" I ask.

"The point is," says Reg, "you can't classify light with any certainty at any exact moment as either a wave or a particle. It's both."

"But that's not a problem," argues Nikki. "It's just the way it is in science. Light doesn't have to be exclusively one or the other."

"That's my point," says Reg. "If we apply either-or thinking that depends on rational certainty to things we can't explain scientifically — like the spiritual realm — it becomes very divisive and even dangerous. It's what we call dualistic or oppositional thinking."

"Because one idea has to be right so the other can be wrong?" asks Tattoo Girl.

Reg nods. "Exactly, so we can put faith in the idea we believe in and exclude the other. Which leads to religious wars and discrimination." He pauses. "And yet, science doesn't have to be dualistic, and we still put credibility in that."

We silently consider this until Free Throw can no longer contain his curiosity. "What does any of that have to do with the cat?"

"The cat," Nikki explains, "was an absurd way of explaining that we can't actually know where probability ends and reality begins. In this hypothetical proposal, you put a cat in a sealed box along with a vial of poison, which can be triggered by a radioactive material." Free Throw cringes but Nikki continues. "However, the exact timing of the radioactive material decaying enough to release the poison and kill the cat cannot be known, so until you open the box there is no way of knowing if the cat is alive or dead."

"Okay," I say, stretching to follow her.

"Except, the cat has to be either alive or dead — there's no other option physically possible — so until you open the box you have to assume that it is both — alive and dead."

"Wow!" That is Tattoo Girl under her breath. I feel the same way. It is all so paradoxical. Maybe that's the point though. Maybe spirituality can be both explicable and inexplicable at the same time.

"Not if the cat's an angel," declares Free Throw, rising.

"Exactly," says Reg, laughing, as we return to work.

But I can't dismiss the conversation completely. Nikki is dedicated to science and rational thought, but even in that realm, there is uncertainty and paradox. Is that so different from the spiritual realm where nothing can be explained with logic or certainty? Reg has even gone so far as to suggest that scientists might understand spiritual concepts better than religious folk because their thinking isn't so dualistic. And if that's the case, Nikki might make a great spiritualist — whatever that is — even without believing in God or religion or intuition. Maybe there's hope for me yet.

Scott barks out orders even more forcefully in the afternoon. Only Catherine responds, working harder and faster. Scott compliments her and I think I see her knees buckle. I look away. We disinfect the pool walls, then leave the pool empty overnight. Reg will come in extra early tomorrow and turn the water on as it will take all day or longer to fill. Tomorrow we'll work on the pool deck, paint the benches and do some work on the shower rooms. At my job that night, I almost fall asleep face down in the cinnamon-sugar.

I can hear the water gushing into the pool as I enter the community centre the next morning. "Does Reg get paid to take us on?" I ask out of curiosity when the others arrive at the shed.

"No," says Tattoo Girl. "And it's Mrs. Stafford who supervises us anyway."

"Really?" I am shocked, but Tattoo Girl speaks with such certainty that I know she's been told this truth by Reg himself. "So, we just work with Reg, but Mrs. Stafford's our official overseer?"

"Correct!" says Tattoo Girl.

"Whoever is responsible for our mandatory community service would have to be approved by the proper authority," Nikki informs us. "Mrs. Stafford likely has that clearance but is too removed from our day-to-day activities here. Hence, Reg."

"Yeah," agrees Tattoo Girl. "It'd have to be that way. They'd never approve Reg on his own."

"Why?" There is something about her statement that sets me on edge.

Tattoo Girl bites her lip, then raises her eyes to the group. "I can tell you something and you won't say anything!" It's not a question.

"Nothing," I promise.

"After all, we are the Nothing Club," confirms Free Throw. We all lean towards Tattoo Girl.

"Reg did time — in prison."

"For what?" we ask in unison.

"He wouldn't say. Just told me what it was like on the inside. He was in for ten years, then got out early for good behaviour."

We stare at each other, and suddenly I know what the conversation under the tree after the Bald Guy incident was about. But this is completely unexpected news, and none of us knows what to make of it.

Before we can speculate on anything, we are interrupted by Catherine's frantic cries. "Quick! Come quick!" She is racing towards us, puffing and gesturing frantically. "Walter's fallen into the pool."

We sprint onto the pool deck; the pool is now partially full of water. The old dog is paddling at the concrete edge of the deep end, his brittle nails scratching at the wall in vain.

"How long has he been in there?" I ask, slipping off my sneakers, depositing my cell phone onto the lifeguard chair and pulling my T-shirt over my head.

"I don't know, but he's getting tired."

That much is obvious and every thirty seconds or so, Walter stops dog paddling and slips beneath the water. He is a lab, so I reckon he's comfortable in the water, but the problem is he's got nowhere to go right now, and I don't know how long he can last.

"Careful," advises Nikki, "it would not be advisable to dive."

I jump into the neck-deep water beside Walter, who immediately paddles towards me, his claws scratching at my legs and arms. "Hey, buddy," I tell him, "we're gonna get you out. Just stay calm." I try to support him, but the best I can do is lean against the pool wall and hold his body up with my legs. The ladder has been removed and taken away for repairs. "Anybody got an idea?" I call up to the others. "He's too heavy for me to lift out."

Free Throw has the long pole used to fish things out of the pool. "Maybe we can slide this under his collar and hoist him out."

I manage to wedge a pole through his collar, but the three of them together can't get enough leverage to lift him.

"There has to be another way," says Tattoo Girl. They all look at Nikki.

"We need an inclined plane," she says.

The dog is tiring, leaning more and more against me. "Okay, well, can we get on that?" I sputter. The water is high enough that I have to bounce off the bottom to keep my head above it.

"The bench," says Nikki, "in the change room. Unscrew the top of it."

"Where are the tools?" asks Free Throw as I submerge momentarily.

Catherine hurries into the pool office, grabs a toolbox and disappears into the change room with Free Throw and Nikki. Tattoo Girl stays at the poolside.

Free Throw re-emerges moments later. "The bolts are rusted," he says from the change room door. "We don't have time."

Walter is in trouble, scratching and whining plaintively. "Stay afloat, boy," I tell him. "Ouch!" A lifeguard ring hits me on the head, and I look up to see Tattoo Girl grinning down at me.

"Put that one around Walter," she instructs me.

Getting a dog into a ring is a challenge, but eventually I manage to pull Walter's front paws through and wedge the ring around his middle. The only problem is that it wants to turn him on his back and when it does, he thrashes like crazy, but at least he can float a little on his own.

"Catch!" cries Tattoo Girl, and a second ring lands close to me. I grab it, hang onto the dog's ring to keep him right side up and float along beside him.

"Okay, that buys us a little time," says Nikki philosophically.

Catherine digs her cell phone out of her pocket and dials. "Yes, I'd like the fire department," she says just as Reg arrives and takes in the whole situation. Closing my eyes, I wonder why I didn't think of that.

Twenty minutes later, I am videoing the firefighters lifting Walter to safety in a large net stretched across the pool and manned by a team of five firefighters. Scott arrives just as the dog, still wearing his lifeguard ring, limps to safety. "What in the hell is going on here?" he demands.

We turn to him and proclaim in unison, "Nothing!"

## CHAPTER 7

Scott is furious. Walter has contaminated the pool water, and it must be treated and cleaned again. "Stupid dog!" he barks, gesturing angrily at all of us as if we are somehow responsible.

Free Throw rubs Walter's ears and consoles the tired dog. Walter will recover with a lot of sleep and attention and there is no danger of not having attention today. Reg checks on the old dog constantly as do all of us members of the Nothing Club. Even Nikki pats the old lab's head awkwardly, then tentatively strokes his ears. "They are exceptionally soft and silky," she observes before pulling her hand away and wiping it on the grass as if to remove all potential fleas. I wonder if it's her first time petting a dog. It certainly isn't Catherine's. She visits Walter numerous times that morning.

"I didn't know you liked animals," I say.

"I have three cats," she tells me. "My parents won't let me have a dog."

"I know that feeling," I tell her.

"Or a horse or a llama or an alpaca," she says, and I have to laugh.

Scott is in a terrible mood all day. He assumes his dictator posture and orders us around with such authority that even Free Throw is starting to get pissed.

"Look, son," says Reg, catching Scott's arm as he throws a hose to the ground. "Getting upset isn't helping any of us. In fact, the more anger and frustration you put out there, the more it'll come right back at you."

Scott yanks his arm free with such force that Reg crashes to the deck. "You're not my boss, old man," he snarls. "Keep your karmic lectures."

We are on our feet, all of us. Nikki, Catherine and I help Reg up while Free Throw moves towards the lifeguard. But Tattoo Girl is closer and before any of us know what has happened, Scott lays in a crumpled heap on the concrete, moaning.

"Are you okay?" queries Reg, back on his feet.

"She kneed me in the groin," says Scott, still writhing.

"Margaret, what happened?" Reg asks.

"Nothing."

That was predictable. I try not to laugh.

Reg frowns at her.

"Okay, I slipped on the water and my knee collided with his balls. It is a pool deck."

Scott swears at her.

"Alright," says Reg, managing to keep a straight face. "I think now's a good time to take lunch. We'll reconvene here in an hour."

Catherine follows Scott to a lounge chair then joins us as we lead Walter back to the garden shed. I snap a photo of her and the dog, but her lunch is in the concession, so she doesn't stay. I wonder if she's headed back to check on Scott. The thought perturbs me although I'm not sure why. We all try to share our lunches with Walter, but he doesn't have much appetite, which worries me. After all, he is a lab.

Nikki is still trying to figure out the relationship between science and the spiritual realm and now, thanks to Scott's comment, the nature of karma. She spends the lunch hour poring over internet sites and interrogating us. "According to this," she tells us, "karma is a cause-and-effect cycle linked to a person's actions; in other words what happens to individuals happens because they cause it to happen with the actions in their life."

"Lives," says Tattoo Girl from behind closed eyes. "Karma doesn't just affect this lifetime. It's linked to all lifetimes."

She says it with such certainty that it makes me wonder how she knows all this stuff, from the Bible to reincarnation.

Nikki puts her phone away. "Assuming we all believe in reincarnation," she says, qualifying Tattoo Girl's statement with a healthy dose of sarcasm, "which of course can't be verified with our five senses . . . which takes me full circle to the beginning."

I dig my heels into the grass and wonder if reincarnation is for real. Maybe Dad will come back as someone else. Maybe I will. If Tattoo Girl's right and karma is legit, I'm screwed. I look around at the Nothing Club. Maybe we all are. Perhaps the others share my thoughts. Tattoo Girl gets to her feet and wanders off without a word. Free Throw leaps up, palms a basketball and shoots hoops without sinking a single one.

I retrieve a ball that comes my way and join him for a few shots. "How about you, Free Throw. You wanna come back as a pro basketball player in your next life?"

He dribbles the ball. "Catholics don't believe in that stuff, Grady . . . but I don't know." He wipes his forehead, and a look of skepticism crosses his face. "Sometimes religion sucks."

"How so?"

"It's so black and white," he says. "I feel like life isn't like that."

"Like there's more grey?"

He nods. I wait for him to go on, but he doesn't. We shoot hoops for a while, then he holds the ball and adds, "Maybe Nikki's right!"

About what? I wonder, but he just dribbles in for a lay-up. I wander back towards the shed and lounge around beside Walter in an oddly introspective and unsettled mood. I'm inclined to take a hard look at my life today. So I stroll towards the children's playground seeking privacy. The summer's been brutal. I mean, I ended up doing community service because . . . I consider the reasons for a moment. Because I didn't have the guts to stand up to Will's know-it-all cousin about setting off fireworks. Then again, neither did Will, but according to his latest texts, he's loving Switzerland, and he's even met some Swiss beauty, although I haven't seen a photo yet. Still, I could have just walked away. Sure, Tyler would have mocked me, but so what? I wouldn't be weeding gardens and cleaning pools with the Nothing Club. I reiterate the thought and my energy sinks at the idea of not being here, not knowing Tattoo Girl or Nikki or Free Throw, Catherine, or Reg. Not rescuing old Walter from the pool. Not having Nikki constantly make me think of things I've never thought to think of. And yet, there's a part of me —

"Shit, Rigoh, I can't." Tattoo Girl's voice reaches me in a heated whisper. She is crouched inside the plastic children's playhouse, on her phone.

I creep closer, as silently as I can, across the recycled rubber tire surface.

"Look, I don't want this anymore." Her words are defiant and strong, but her voice is fragile. She lets her head fall onto her forearms, and I watch her ink-black hair move back and forth as if she is swaying in her resolve. "I don't know, Rigoh." She stretches her tattooed legs out in front of her. "No don't come here. Reg will call the cops." She pauses. "I'll meet you at the Sugar Shack at five." She hangs up, groans and leans back against the playhouse wall.

I creep to the edge of the playground, then sprint to the shed, pausing only long enough to acknowledge Free Throw's rabbit friends. "Free Throw! Nikki!" I call as I reach them.

"What's up?" asks Free Throw stopping mid-shot. He tucks the ball under his arm and strides towards me.

I tell them about Rigoh and Tattoo Girl. "We can't let her go. This guy's bad news."

Free Throw nods in agreement. "Real bad news," he echoes.

"Shall we ask Reg to intervene?" asks Nikki. "It proved effective last time."

I shake my head. "Reg can control what happens on this property, but this is out of his territory."

"How about a little heart-to-heart when she gets back?" suggests Free Throw.

"Maybe." But my gut's telling me that's the wrong thing to do. Besides, then she'd know I'd eavesdropped on her. "Or what do you say we just show up at the Sugar Shack just before five. I mean it's a free country, right?"

Nikki is searching on her phone. "What," she asks finally, "is a Sugar Shack? It doesn't appear in the city directory."

Free Throw grins at her. "Just the biggest candy store in the country. You never been?"

Nikki shakes her head.

"You've never had blue whales?"

"Blue whales?"

"And sour watermelons? Or fuzzy peaches?"

Nikki is frantically typing.

"Stop!" I say grabbing her phone from her. "Tonight, you get to indulge in sweetness at its finest." I can hardly wait to take Nikki into the Sugar Shack and watch her eyes pop out of her head. There is literally a half-kilometre of candy bins in that store — every sugary, gummy, sweet, gooey treat you can imagine. If we can get her past the idea of ingesting food colouring, she's going to love it.

"I have a commitment at five o'clock," she says, and I can tell by her voice that she is genuinely disappointed. "My violin lesson."

I kick a patch of grass between two sidewalk blocks. "Can't you take a rain check this once?" I ask. "For Tattoo Girl?"

"Unfortunately, no. My father would be incredibly disappointed in me as would my teacher."

"What if you were sick or sprained a hand?" I suggest. "You wouldn't be able to go then."

"But I'm not."

"You could be."

"If I miss my lesson because I am ill, I will be quarantined for three days."

I gulp. That is a little extreme.

She furrows her forehead. "On the other hand, if my violin teacher were unable to attend, then I could call and say we had to work late, on account of the dog."

"That's brilliant!" I exclaim. Then, I think for a moment. Getting Nikki fake sick or keeping her late is one thing. Delaying her violin teacher is another. "Isn't that a little beyond our control?"

Nikki is scheming. "Right before he comes to our house, he teaches Roger at the university in the music laboratory." Her fingers are moving so quickly that I can hardly see them. "The door has one of those computer code locks and last night, some security glitch scrambled the codes, so they're on manual right now." My brain hurts trying to follow hers. "If I can hack in and set those manual codes to change after my instructor's in, it will take security at least half an hour to figure it out. By which time, my lesson will no longer be feasible."

"Okay," says Free Throw in a voice that confirms he has understood as much as I have.

"Wait," I say, "you've already been nailed once for hacking. If they catch you again . . ."

Nikki dismisses me. "Anybody could alter the codes. They won't trace it. Besides, I'll manufacture a remote location." Her eyes flit rapidly as she works.

Free Throw and I leave her to it as Tattoo Girl joins us. She is reserved and heavily veiled like she was the first day I met her. Only then do I realize that over the past few weeks, she's gradually uncloaked herself. I say nothing about the conversation, only watch Nikki, who finally whispers, "Done," just before lunch ends. "Ideally," she tells me, "I should get a call by four twenty-five. At that point, my violin instructor will be unable to reach our house with enough time for a reasonable lesson before he must depart for his subsequent one."

A yoga mat hits me in the side of the head, as Free Throw distributes them. Reg isn't back yet, but I find an online meditation site and synch my phone to the speaker. We all settle into our meditation. At one point, I think I hear footsteps, but then I focus on my breathing and return to my place of stillness. This time I stay there longer before I am distracted. When the meditation ends, we roll up the mats and head back to the pool.

"My body experienced a tangible reduction in heart rate today," comments Nikki. "Brainwave patterns may also have altered."

"No shit!" says Tattoo Girl, but her voice is not as harsh as her words.

The afternoon seems to drag on forever. Scott is less than pleased that we are late, but Reg just smiles when we tell him we had to meditate. Catherine feels caught in the middle, Tattoo Girl is preoccupied, and Nikki watches the clock incessantly. Reg is concerned about Walter, who is still refusing to eat. I suggest that that might be because he can't eat in his sleep, but reconsider. Labs probably can. It is 4:17 by the time we gather our stuff and get ready to leave. Tattoo Girl splits right away while the rest of us hang around the pool. By 4:25, no call has come on Nikki's phone. "Maybe Free Throw and I ought to head over there," I suggest. "Do you still have time to get home?"

But Nikki isn't listening. At 4:27 the phone rings. Nikki takes the call, but I am distracted by the pool alarm blaring loudly. Nikki puts one hand over her ear to block out the raging alarm as Reg hustles towards us. "Must be a low battery," he says. "I'll have to override the alarm." We hear the alarm die then Reg rejoins us.

"There are many inventors working on creating a battery with a longer power source," Nikki advises. "Such an invention would have a massive impact on society and be of great assistance to all humanity."

"Well," I say jokingly, "why don't you invent one?"

She frowns. "My father made the same suggestion," she tells me, and I sense he wasn't joking. She sighs. "However, I seem incapable of inventing anything that would alleviate human suffering or significantly change our lives."

"Well," says Reg softly, "you know what they say. Change your thoughts, change your life." He turns and saunters away, leaving Nikki looking both puzzled and intrigued.

"Change your thoughts, change your life," echoes Nikki.

"Does that imply that I can create reality with my thoughts just by —"

"Come on," says Free Throw. "We need to hurry."

Soon, the three of us are hustling towards the Sugar Shack. I spot Tattoo Girl sitting on one of the benches outside, waiting. We head straight for her.

"Hey," I say, trying to sound nonchalant.

She leaps to her feet, the two leopards tattooed on her thigh baring their teeth with her movement. "What are you doing here?"

"Can you believe that Nikki's never had a blue whale?" I say lamely.

Tattoo Girl pins me to the bench with her eyes. "Don't mess with me, Grady."

I come clean. "Okay, I accidentally overheard you talking to Rigoh." Her facial muscles tense.

"You can walk away," says Free Throw.

Tattoo Girl spins on her heel, then glares at us. "It's not that easy," she spits. "Besides, they're my group, you know, who I hang with."

"You can hang with us," I suggest. She gives me a lips-only smile. "Come on," I say, "we're not that bad. I mean this is a pretty exclusive membership. Not everyone gets to be in the Nothing Club."

"You have to be nothing, man," says Free Throw. "I mean a real no-good-for-nothing, waste-of-a-human-being sort. That ain't easy."

"With mandatory community service," adds Nikki. "We have strict criteria."

For a moment Tattoo Girl wavers. I see Rigoh's black pickup truck pull up on an adjacent street.

"Total losers," I tell her, "without a single redeeming quality . . . well except maybe a soft spot for dogs."

"And an intense dislike for arrogant lifeguards," says Nikki.

Tattoo Girl laughs. Rigoh honks the horn, but Tattoo Girl is still standing with us, so I keep talking. "And with an ex-con as a boss."

Tattoo Girl's eyes meet mine, and I see a flash of disappointment. "I have to go," she says, and strides towards the truck.

We watch for a moment, our spirits plunging. My thoughts follow Tattoo Girl into the pickup and from there ... who knows? She doesn't look at us as it pulls away. We stand mutely in front of the store until Nikki exclaims, "Can we still go in?"

The look on Nikki's face is all that I thought it would be, but it doesn't bring me the joy I thought it would. Not knowing that Tattoo Girl couldn't be dissuaded. Still, I show Nikki the fuzzy peaches and pour a few into a small white bag. And then the sweetness of the moment displaces the disappointment, and we fill bag after bag. Nikki is like a child in a candy store. We consume enough sweets to make all three of us sick.

## CHAPTER 8

But I am truly sick on Monday when I see Tattoo Girl's face. No amount of makeup can hide the black eye and stormy bruise on her temple.

Free Throw turns away when he catches sight of her and Nikki's face pales.

"I fell down the stairs," Tattoo Girl declares when I am unable to look away.

Into Rigoh's fist, I want to add. Tattoo Girl's veil is tightly drawn around her. Reg inhales sharply when he sees her, then announces that the meditation session will be longer today. And he insists that Tattoo Girl help him with the yoga mats.

"She looks rough," I say under my breath as she reluctantly disappears into the shed.

"Nobody deserves that!" Free Throw mutters, wringing his hands. He is visibly distressed.

"You okay, man?" I ask.

He bends, bracing his arms on his knees as if recovering from a sprint. "Yeah, no, I mean, it's just that when my dad drinks too much, sometimes, he . . ." His voice falters.

I put a hand on his shoulder. "Your mom?" I ask tentatively.

"Billy!" he says, his voice cracking.

Nikki's face is a ghostly white. She winds her shoulder-length hair into a tight knot and glances at the shed. "Why does she stay?"

I study Tattoo Girl's slim, inked form then glance at Free Throw again, wondering how he, his mom and his faith make sense of his home situation. "I'm guessing it's complicated," I respond, but just the thought makes me nauseous.

The afternoon is brutally hot, and humid. Tattoo Girl is hurting outside and inside. Her skin reeks of alcohol and she is obviously hungover. There's no way I want to dig gardens alongside her in this burning heat. Luckily, I don't have to because, after lunch, Reg greets us all with a box of emerald green T-shirts.

"Courtesy of the Canadian Diabetes Association," Mrs. Stafford says, appearing behind us. She grimaces as she takes in Tattoo Girl's shiner and glances meaningfully at Reg before joining us in the courtyard. Recomposing herself, she fills us in. "This week is Diabetes Awareness Week and you four are going to be ambassadors." As it turns out, being an ambassador means educating the public about diabetes from the shade of a gigantic umbrella, so we're in.

Our first afternoon is spent with Mrs. Stafford, who gives us the lowdown on diabetes — how you get it, the difference between Types 1 and 2, how you treat it, along with a testing and injection demonstration, current research and statistics and information about how to prevent Type 2 diabetes. I can't help thinking that Mrs. Stafford and Adrianna were pretty unfortunate to have Type 1, but I admire her for wanting to educate the rest of us who were luckier. We feel pretty confident by the time we take our spots in the shade of canopies bearing the CDA logo the next morning, on the first of the free swim days that Mrs. Stafford sponsors. Free Throw's and my table has four popular beverages and the question

"Which of these contains the most sugar?" Nikki and Tattoo Girl's stand, with four snack bars, has the same question. Everyone who guesses gets a free balloon animal: squirrels, rabbits, mice, alligators — we have a whole box full.

"Where'd you get all these balloon animals?" Tattoo Girl asks Mrs. Stafford as she comes by to check on us.

"Reg."

"Where'd Reg get 'em?"

"He made them," she says. We are all caught off guard by her response, but as soon as we see him, we beg him for a demonstration.

He fashions an elephant for Free Throw's little sister who has her fifth birthday today. "Where'd you learn to do that?" I ask but then I know the answer. Reg smiles and doesn't respond. I think it was a good use of his time and wonder again what he was in for.

Catherine brings us all slushies at Mrs. Stafford's request, and we slurp noisily, trying not to think about their sugar content, then fill Walter's dish with rainbow liquid. The concession is busy, but Catherine hangs around for a bit anyway, then rushes back in to serve the kajillion kids. During lunch she brings Scott a slushie. He jumps off his lifeguard perch and gives her a fake white smile designed to melt the ice in the drink. Catherine scurries back to the concession with a vivid blush. My stomach turns.

Our routine will be the same all week. Our job is to educate kids, adults and whoever else shows up, about diabetes and field the questions they ask. "I know being low is dangerous, but what happens when your blood sugars get too high?" I ask Mrs. Stafford.

"If they are consistently on the high side, then eventually people with diabetes can suffer with everything from blindness to heart disease later in life."

I look twice at the puffed rice square I am eating, remembering that marshmallows are pretty much pure sugar. "Don't worry," she reassures me, "your pancreas will take care of that."

For the first time in my life, I don't take my health for granted.

On Tuesday I stop to say hello to Catherine and notice something. Her eyes are a different colour — a translucent blue, and she's not wearing her glasses. "Weren't your eyes green yesterday?" I ask her.

"Contacts," she says nodding. "They change the colour of my eyes."

"Why would you want to do that?"

"Blue eyes are so much nicer," she replies as I blink my own extraordinarily ordinary hazel ones. Her gaze drifts to the lifeguard chair, and I seem to recall that Scott has striking cobalt-blue eyes.

I confirm that is the case later that day when Scott drops a map drawn on a napkin onto the counter in front of Catherine while I'm buying a Fudgesicle. "I'm having a barbecue and party Friday," he tells her, shouldering past me. "Come by after work." He winks at her and I stare stunned.

"You going to go?" I ask her tersely.

Catherine shrugs. "Are you?" She folds the napkin in half and tucks it into her purple handbag.

"I wasn't invited."

"I wouldn't go if you paid me," says Tattoo Girl, coming up behind me.

We collect our frozen treats and leave. "Actually, I'm shocked," I tell Tattoo Girl as we meander back to our umbrellas. "She doesn't exactly seem like his type."

"She's not but she adores him, and he knows it."

For the second time that week, I feel sick to my stomach.

The feeling returns every time Catherine blinks her newly blue eyes.

But the changes don't stop there. On Wednesday, Tattoo Girl uses the change room before the pool has opened for the day and returns to the shed with a perplexed look on her face. "Guess what I found in the little girls' room?" she says. She pulls a shopping bag from beneath her arm and shakes out a short grey fashionable skirt and an almost see-through pale blue shirt trimmed with lace."

"Whose are those?" I ask.

"Mine now," says Tattoo Girl, but we can all tell that she doesn't mean it. "If nobody claims them."

"The locker rooms are cleaned every night. Those must have been put there this morning," deduces Nikki, "which could only mean that they belong to —"

"Catherine!" we all exclaim.

"Pretty sexy for concession girl," observes Tattoo Girl, but as soon as she mentions Catherine, we see her figure weaving tentatively towards us.

"Hey, Catherine," I say, smiling broadly. "What brings you out to the Nothing Club headquarters?"

"Um, I, uh, left a bag of clothes in the girls' change room and I was wondering —"

Before she can finish, Tattoo Girl tosses her the bag. Catherine catches it against her stomach. "Nice," offers Tattoo Girl.

"Thanks," murmurs Catherine, then unexpectedly plunks down on the grass next to Free Throw. "My grandmother died Sunday," she says just like that, leaving us all wide-eyed.

"Aw," says Free Throw. "I'm sorry."

"That's tough," I add. "Had she been sick?"

Catherine tugs on a blade of grass. "Apparently, she had leukemia, but she didn't really believe in doctors and western medicine. It wasn't her way." She looks up at us and explains. "Her ancestors were from the Siksika Nation."

"I didn't know you're Indigenous," I say.

"Well, just my grandmother was, so I'm part Siksika."

"Cool," adds Free Throw.

"Mmm, we used to collect herbs and medicinal plants together," Catherine says. A smile parts her lips. "My grandparents had this great farm. We loved the woods and the creek and all their animals." She grins. "And we had this awesome fort in the hayloft."

"Where was it?" I ask.

"East of the city near Ridgeview."

Free Throw bumps her shoulder again in an oddly affectionate gesture.

"When's the funeral?" I ask.

"Saturday, but I don't want to go."

Who does? A shiver runs down my back and suddenly I am transported to my father's funeral. It's a blur really — the coffin carried by six firefighters in uniform, his captain's eulogy, hymns, prayers, candles flickering — all a blur except for the woman with the red curly hair. She approaches my mother at the end of the service, clutching a sleeping baby in her arms. She lost her husband in the fire. Dad wasn't able to save him; the floor gave out beneath the two of them. He saved her and the baby first, then handed them off to his colleague before going back in. She and Mom share a tearful embrace at the back of the church, and her face is forever imprinted on my memory.

"Your parents going to be okay with you not going?" asks Free Throw, interrupting my reverie. "It's when the soul returns home, you know?"

"No," says Catherine, and I'm not sure which part of Free Throw's questions she's answering, "but I don't care. My brother's in Florida at a robotics conference. He won't come back for it." She rises to her feet and brushes off her backside. "Thanks," she says gratefully and heads back to the concession carrying the shopping bag.

"That sucks," says Free Throw.

"Yeah," I agree.

Tattoo Girl watches her go. "Those clothes ain't for no funeral."

Reg arrives and we go back to work as diabetes ambassadors. The energy of the day is odd though, out of place, like the universe is out of order somehow. It really goes downhill over lunch. We are sitting around the shed with Walter when I hear three long whistles. "Did anyone hear that?" I ask.

Tattoo Girl nods and Free Throw shakes his head. "Probably just someone calling a dog," he says when it comes again, but his sunny optimism has faded. A few minutes later he excuses himself to go to the washroom.

We are all on our feet within seconds. "Give him a minute," Tattoo Girl advises us. "Then follow me."

We do, moving stealthily across the field and ducking behind a portable storage unit when we see Free Throw in conversation with an older version of himself. "His brother Billy," Tattoo Girl tells us. Billy half-hangs on Free Throw, his head bobbing, his voice rising and falling. Suddenly he clenches Free Throw's shoulders and shakes him violently. I resist the urge to rush from our hiding place behind the hedge.

"He needs a fix," Tattoo Girl informs us, restraining me with her hand. "He wants money."

Reluctantly, Free Throw reaches into his shorts pocket and pulls out some folded bills. He never has money, and I know this was planned. His brother snatches it from Free Throw's hands and stumbles away. Free Throw's shoulders slump. His head droops and he stands perfectly still. Slowly he folds his hands, then turns and starts to sing something that sounds like a psalm, extending his arms. I wonder if he's praying for his brother or asking forgiveness for himself? Or worrying that God will strike them both down? Soon he is turning in circles, moving like a bird in the air, buoying himself up to that place of happiness he occupies. I can't help remembering his desire to be an eagle.

"His brother's an addict," Tattoo Girl explains, shattering my musings and answering Nikki's wordless questions.

We scurry back to the shed and try to look as if nothing has happened when Free Throw returns. But something has.

I have trouble losing myself in meditation that afternoon; there are so many unanswered questions. Questions about God and pain and forgiveness and life after death and more. I package all those things into a symbolic hot-air balloon and set it adrift. Then I refocus on my breathing. Finally, my breath slows and becomes automatic. A calmness surrounds me, and I feel a growing sense of peace. The chimes sound twice.

I swing by the concession later that day. "Hey, Catherine," I say, leaning over the counter. "How's it going?"

"Okay," she says. A torn magazine page lays on the counter between us.

"Who's that?" I ask, pointing at some voluptuous model wearing a sequined gold dress.

She folds the paper and slips it into her purse. "I was just thinking of having my hair cut like hers," she says timidly.

For Scott? I wonder. I force a smile to my lips. "You'll be a whole different person tomorrow."

She blushes. "My appointment isn't until Friday."

I return to my umbrella feeling edgy and irritated. Where has the calm of my meditation gone?

Things get worse when Mrs. Stafford, busy handing out brochures and educating young parents about diabetes, collapses, smashing down on the concrete courtyard. Free Throw and Nikki reach her first. Her breathing is shallow and her face bright red. I call 911. She clutches her elbow and moans. Reg arrives before the paramedics and insists on going to the hospital with her. We watch them strap her to the stretcher and disappear into the white box van. "I'll let you know as soon as I know something," calls Reg. "The paramedics think it's probably just a little angina."

"Nikki Wiki?" asks Tattoo Girl, making reference to our walking encyclopedia friend. I know the name will stick.

"A condition marked by severe pain in the chest, often spreading to the shoulders, arms and neck, caused by an inadequate blood supply." That sounds serious. "The emergency personnel will check her heart and circulation."

For the next two hours, we continue handing out brochures and balloon animals, but without our earlier enthusiasm. What's taking Reg so long? I wonder. What are they doing at the hospital?

"It's her heart," Reg tells us when he returns to the pool just before home time. "They've got her on medication now and the cardiologist will see her tomorrow."

"That woman's got a big heart," observes Free Throw.

"And she's broken her elbow. She must have cracked it on the pavement when she fell. She'll need surgery, which is complicated by her diabetes and now, her heart." His eyes betray his concern. "I'm going over to her place to pick up some things she needs and then back to the hospital." He heads towards the house, then calls over his shoulder. "I'm not sure if I'll be here first thing tomorrow, but I'll call Catherine. If I'm not, well, use your heads."

I cycle faster than usual the next morning and arrive early, but Catherine is already at the bike rack, locking up her bicycle. "I'm really sorry about your grandmother," I say as we stroll towards the centre. "It sounds like you have lots of good memories of her."

Her sneakers squeak on the concrete blocks. "My brother and I used to spend our summers with my grandparents, without our parents. The hayloft was our sanctuary, complete with cookies and water pistols." She smiles, but then the light in her eyes dims.

"Have you decided about the funeral?" I ask her.

"My dad's convinced I'm going." I wait hoping she'll go on. "My parents want a traditional Christian funeral; my grandmother converted when she met my grandfather." She hesitates. "But after he died five years ago, she returned to her Indigenous ways. I don't think she ever truly wanted to give them up."

I wonder what that must be like — to surrender your spiritual beliefs and embrace someone else's.

"I've learned so much about her people and their ways in the last few years, and I just know she wouldn't want the sort of funeral my dad is planning. But he won't listen to me, and he doesn't even want to mention her First Nations heritage. I think his business analyst persona is embarrassed by his Indigenous roots."

I feel for her. Funerals are tough enough without that kind of underlying tension.

The others arrive moments later, before our designated start time. Even Free Throw is early. Maybe it's our curiosity, maybe it's because we want to be above suspicion, maybe it's because we know Reg won't be there. "He was here earlier to feed Penny and Walter, but he's gone back up to the hospital this morning," Catherine informs us, carrying a note he left in her cash drawer.

We run the diabetes booths. Halfway through the day, a kids' day camp arrives with their counsellor. Bridget is a knockout, especially in her bikini, and Free Throw and I can't help salivating over her on the pool deck. Neither can Scott. And Catherine can't keep her eyes off the two of them. Mid-afternoon, Catherine takes Scott a cold pop, which he promptly shares with Bridget. By the time Reg's call comes and Catherine relays the message that Reg will be in later that day, she is visibly on edge.

I think it would be nice to console her, but I don't know what to say. Tattoo Girl does. "He's a dick," Tattoo Girl tells Catherine, jerking her thumb at Scott, who is practically draped over Bridget. I'm wondering how many small children might have drowned this afternoon. Catherine's blue eyes blink rapidly before she retreats to the concession.

"Mrs. Stafford will have an angioplasty as soon as they have a spot in the operating room," Reg tells us when he arrives.

"A thin tube with a small balloon attached to it is inserted into a blood vessel usually in the thigh," explains Nikki, with no prompting. "Then the doctor inflates the balloon so any plaque causing a blockage becomes dislodged, and blood flow is improved." She pauses then adds in a tired voice, "My mother has recently conducted a study on the effectiveness of this technique in patients with blood cancers."

The way she says it makes me wonder if her parents also grew up with outrageous expectations and pressures.

"It might take a few days until the surgeon can schedule her," Reg says. "They tell me it's common surgery and quite safe. Once they know what's going on with her heart, they'll operate on her elbow."

I imagine sitting in a hospital room with broken bones waiting for an operating room to come free and cringe at the thought of the pain.

"Can we see her?" asks Free Throw.

Reg looks surprised. "Yeah, I guess. She can have four visitors at any given time." He smiles and I know he appreciates the offer. "She's at the Rocky Ridge Hospital. Unit 81."

We decide to go after work that night. Nikki's violin lessons are cancelled while her instructor is on holiday, and Free Throw's aunt has agreed to stay late to babysit his siblings. Tattoo Girl doesn't have to let anybody know. I call Mom and she is thrilled to see my compassionate side surface.

On the way in, we stop at the floral shop, pool our money and buy a small African violet with soft mauve blossoms. Mrs. Stafford is surprised and truly delighted to see us. "Did Reg make you come?" she asks with a laugh.

"No," we blurt out simultaneously, sounding as if he did but knowing that he will tell her it was our idea anyway. For the next twenty minutes or so, we amuse her with tales of the pool and the funny questions we've been asked at the booths. She tells us how bad the food is and shows us the X-rays. There is a wide gap in the elbow bones. When supper arrives, we take our leave; all the way down on the elevator, we are surrounded by a collective warmth.

"Is this inexplicable feeling something spiritual?" Nikki asks as we descend.

We all laugh as Free Throw reaches out to hug her.

## CHAPTER 9

Reg shows up on time the next day and it is business as usual. Bridget is back with her camp kids and Scott is fixated on her. By the end of the day, they are inseparable, and Catherine is trying to be emotionless. I do my best to distract her as Scott catches Bridget against the fence and locks lips with her, but Catherine has already seen them. She gathers her things from the concession, then waits outside the pool entrance, stoic and silent as the last of the poolgoers take their leave. Free Throw, Nikki and Tattoo Girl are just finishing up at the shed, but I know they'll be here soon. I lean my bike against the fence and join Catherine on the curb. We are waiting for an update from Reg, who has taken a run up to the hospital.

"Have you got plans for the weekend?" I ask Catherine. She fiddles with a zipper on her pack, then grimaces. "Other than your grandmother's funeral," I add, mentally kicking myself for not remembering earlier. I change the subject. "I thought Reg would be back by now."

She glances at her phone. "Me too. I've got an appointment in twenty minutes."

"You should go," I tell her. "I'll wait and then text you."

But Catherine does not respond. She is staring sideways at Scott, who is standing with his arm around Bridget's shoulders at the edge of the parking lot while she texts. I throw stones at the garbage can in an effort to garner Catherine's attention. Clang! She glances at me, then unravels a thread of her fraying jean shorts as the couple disappears hand in hand.

The others arrive. We sit, the five of us on the curb, waiting for Reg. Finally, his red hatchback pulls into the parking lot. "No change; she's stable and awaiting surgery," he reports, getting out with Penny in his arms. I've completely forgotten about Mrs. Stafford's dogs, but thankfully Reg hasn't. "Looks like you guys are done for the week." Reg grins. "By the way, all she could talk about was your visit."

"You visited?" asks Catherine. She adds sadly, "Without me?"

"Sorry," says Free Throw. "We didn't think. I mean, it was just the Nothing Club, you know." And after that, there's nothing to say.

Penny squirms and Reg sets her down.

Free Throw whistles and she yaps joyfully, then jumps onto his lap.

"Is there any way one of you could keep Penny for the weekend? I can't have dogs at my apartment. There's a dog door and an automatic feeder at the house so I could leave her there with Walter, but I think Penny's a little rattled without Mrs. Stafford." Reg is technically addressing all of us, but really, we all know who Penny loves most. Free Throw!

"I'd love to," he tells Reg.

Reg unloads an ice cream bucket of dog food and treats and passes them to Free Throw, along with Penny's collar and leash. "She sleeps on the bed," he says a little apologetically.

"Of course, she does," replies Free Throw, clipping her

onto the leash and bouncing away from us. Tattoo Girl falls into step beside them. I watch enviously.

Catherine stands, slipping her lilac purse over her shoulder and hoisting her backpack with her other hand. But before she can take a step, the pool alarm blares. She frowns. "I set it just like you showed me," she informs Reg, who is already hustling towards the office. She hurries after him, and Nikki and I take our leave, me pushing my bike, Nikki walking with purposeful strides, Penny prancing ahead of us in the distance.

Nikki is deep in thought. "I confess that I know little about animals," she says finally, "but based on my observations, there seems to be a great deal of positive — maybe even spiritual — energy associated with their presence in humans' lives. And Free Throw, well, he appears to have an uncanny ability to communicate with animal species that inhabit this earth. Or am I mistaken?"

"Nope, you got that right," I say. "You're really intrigued by this stuff, hey?"

"I have spent days reading on the law of attraction, spirituality, karma, vibrations, intuition and more."

"And?"

She presses her fingertips together. "I continue to find nothing definitive, and yet, I cannot deny the presence of something positive associated with this inexplicable domain, at least on an anecdotal level. But I still require scientific evidence to support my observations."

We have reached her bus stop. "Well then," I quip sassily, straddling my bike and echoing Reg's words, "maybe you need to change your frame of reference." I pedal away before she can close her lower jaw.

Wandering home, I am lost in thought. Only I'm not lost because suddenly I know where I am — in front of a recently constructed house just blocks from my own. The little girl is probably five or six now, and she and her red-haired mother are planting flowers in the front yard. I stop in front of the house, without even realizing I've stopped. I can't remember what it looked like before the fire, even though I'm sure I biked past it to soccer practice. But I can still close my eyes and see the charred remains after the firefighters had left. Mom, Charlotte and I came to see it on Christmas Day. Dad's graveyard. Natural cremation. There wasn't much left of his body — his watch and wedding ring. His colleagues from the station delivered them to us a few days later. Ashes to ashes. I think I prefer dust to dust!

The little girl's flowered hat half-covers thin strawberry blond curls and I wonder if her father was blond as well. Mine wasn't. I got my light brown wavy hair from him. I wish I'd inherited his muscular build. The child glances up suddenly and so does her mother, squinting as if she recognizes me. I ride away. I don't want them to know me. It will be harder to hate them if they do.

Nikki sends the word out first. She was playing around listening to the police radio channel early Saturday morning and caught Catherine's name. Apparently, she didn't come home last night, and Reg is at the police station.

"What?" I yell into the phone even though she's texted me and I'm hardly awake. Immediately I text then call Catherine but there is no response. We agree to meet at the pool at nine — all four of us — and to keep trying to reach her, only we can't. It is too early for Tattoo Girl to have applied all her eye makeup and she looks surprisingly pretty and feminine without it.

"She's probably just couch surfing at a friend's," says Tattoo Girl, yawning, "to avoid the funeral." She looks slightly miffed at being awakened early on a weekend. "But what's weird is that they took Reg in."

Nikki agrees. "Especially since they wouldn't even treat her like a missing person until twenty-four hours have passed." Nikki's already tracked Reg's unlisted number down and told us there's no answer. We head for the police station. He's there and after some heavy-duty pleading and tears-on-demand from Tattoo Girl, the officer in charge lets us see Reg for three minutes, no more.

"Why are you here?" we ask in unison as we enter the room, where he is seated with a coffee in hand.

"It's a long story," says Reg. He asks the officer to retrieve a silver key on a Glenmeadows Community key chain from his belongings, and the cop disappears into another room, then returns with the key in hand. "It's Mrs. Stafford's. I think she has everything she needs at the moment, but in the event that there's anything she requires from her house . . ." He hesitates. "I'm trusting you. You hang onto it, Grady."

My hand trembles as I sign for the key.

"So what happened?" asks Tattoo Girl in that no-nonsense tone she uses when she wants to cut through all the crap.

Reg breathes deeply and begins in a voice that tells us he's told this same account a dozen times already. "The alarm system at the pool has been malfunctioning. It went off just after you and Free Throw left," he tells Tattoo Girl. Nikki and I nod in confirmation. "Catherine and I went into the office to check on it. I think it must be a faulty wire. I overrode the alarm, then Catherine said she had to leave because she was late to an engagement. So I offered to drive her and she accepted."

"Drive her where?" I ask.

"To Scott's."

"Scott's?" asks Free Throw.

**THE NOTHING CLUB**

"Apparently there was some big party there last night." Reg's voice betrays his confusion.

"That's right," I concur, glancing at Tattoo Girl. "We were there when he invited her earlier this week." The hair on the back of my neck bristles.

"I dropped her off at Scott's, then drove to my apartment." He pauses. "Catherine's parents called the police when she didn't come home Friday night, and they couldn't reach her cell phone. I have an unlisted number, but I'm an emergency contact for the pool, so the police called me early this morning. I came in right away."

So Reg is here voluntarily. "Why are they holding you?" asks Tattoo Girl.

"They aren't holding me exactly. But I was the last one to see Catherine." His voice drops. "So they might want me to make a statement."

"You mean Scott didn't see her?" I ask, my mind spinning.

"Apparently not. The police spoke to Catherine's mom and dad this morning. All they know is that she left for work Friday morning, and they haven't had any contact with her since. They also spoke to Scott. He claims she never showed up at the party."

A bizarre sense of urgency envelops me. Something doesn't add up. The officer advises us that our time is up. He asks us if we have any idea where Catherine might have gone last night — friends or acquaintances, potential romantic interests we know of? But we have nothing to offer. He already knows about Scott. He gives us the pat line and tells us that we know where to find him if we remember anything, before glancing suspiciously at Reg.

"They don't have anything on you," Tattoo Girl whispers.

Reg sighs. "I know, but I'm happy to co-operate. It will all get sorted out. I just hope Catherine's okay." We shuffle awkwardly. "Thanks for looking after Walter and Penny," he says, "and do me a favour if you see Mrs. Stafford . . . don't tell her I'm here, okay?"

"Sure," we murmur.

"If we see her, we shall inform her that you are feeling unwell, possibly the flu and, therefore, are unable to visit," says Nikki. "You can't risk contamination."

"Thank you," says Reg and he reaches out to squeeze our hands.

"So, what do we do now?" asks Free Throw once we're outside the station.

"Wait!" I say. I am at a loss as to why Reg is still at the station or where Catherine might be, but there is nothing we can do at the moment.

"If anybody hears anything, I need to hear it first," instructs Tattoo Girl. She would, I suspect, make a very good dictator. We head in opposite directions, but it is less than three hours before Nikki calls me.

# CHAPTER 10

"The police have named Reg as a person of interest in Catherine's disappearance."

"How do you know?"

"Police radios. The question is why?" Nikki fires back.

This time we meet in Mrs. Stafford's backyard gazebo. Free Throw lopes across the grass to join us with Penny in his arms. "What's up?" he asks.

We all look at Nikki. She's the brains of the operation. She summarizes the information she's garnered so far from the police channel. "It hasn't yet been twenty-four hours since Catherine was last seen, and they haven't officially opened a missing persons file, but they are now detaining Reg." She falls silent, then adds. "I am unable to reach a logical conclusion about the precise meaning of these events."

Just then her phone lights up. She plugs in her earbuds and holds up an open palm. We bite down on our responses and wait, but her expression gives nothing away. Finally, she removes her earbuds, and I can see her eyes flit right and left as if she is filing this new data away before she speaks. "Catherine's glasses were found in the parking lot outside Reg's apartment," she tells us in a sober voice. "They are considering charging Reg with abduction."

"What?" I ask. "That's ludicrous!"

"Why would her glasses be at Reg's place?" asks Free Throw. "He dropped her at Scott's."

"She wears contacts," I announce to nobody in particular. "In fact, she just got new ones." I can feel my angst rising. "This is outrageous, absolutely absurd." I wave both hands in the air as I feel myself slip towards panic. "Why would Reg possibly abduct Catherine?"

"Why do fifty-year-old men abduct teenagers?" asks Tattoo Girl glibly. "What?" she says when we all stare accusingly at her. "I lived on the streets for six months. It happens."

I sink onto the lawn furniture. I can't go there. None of us can.

Tattoo Girl's dragon steadies my shoulder. "Breathe," she instructs, and I do. In for a count of four, then out for eight, just like Reg taught us. She relaxes her grip and then returns to the task at hand. "Now how do we prove Reg's innocence?"

"Logic dictates that our best line of defence for Reg is to find Catherine, so she can, hopefully, corroborate his story, as well as prove that she was not abducted," Nikki states.

"Will," I say, then add, "*will* corroborate his story."

We sit in the gazebo, trying to make sense of everything that feels so wrong. My thoughts swirl dangerously, threatening to pull me under, but I hold my panic at bay with every breath.

"Okay," says Nikki finally, taking charge. "Our first priority is to track Catherine down by retracing her steps starting from the time we last saw her. That was at the pool when she and Reg went to check on the alarm. Correct, Grady?"

"Correct."

"And then Reg drove her to Scott's," adds Free Throw.

"I can't believe she actually went to his party," I say.

Nikki consults her smartphone. "Scott's address is 145 Vale Boulevard, only a kilometre and a half northwest of here. I suggest we check it out and try to put ourselves into Catherine's mindset as best we can."

That proves incredibly difficult, and I suddenly wonder how we could have spent so much time working at the same location this summer and know so little about her. But then she is the girl who wants to be invisible. Or at least she was until Scott came along. We head north in silence. "Why would she go to Scott's party after he left with Bridget?" I know I've said it before, but I just can't get my head around that decision.

"Maybe she went seeking revenge on our playboy lifeguard," purports Tattoo Girl.

"Are you suggesting she attended Scott's party with the intention of trying to harm?" asks Nikki. "That seems very aggressive, totally out of character for the somewhat demure Catherine."

"Those clothes weren't exactly demure," I note. "And she did get contacts as well last week."

"Maybe she was undergoing a transformation," Nikki offers. "A sort of makeover to attract his attention. Eyes, clothes and hair are often common —"

"That's it!" I can hardly contain my excitement. "Catherine had a hair appointment Friday. She showed me a picture of the style she wanted last week." I think back to my last conversation with her on the curb. "And just before Reg arrived, she said she had an appointment in twenty minutes. It must have been her haircut."

"Likely," agrees Tattoo Girl. She has taken off her denim jacket in the summer sun and is wearing a plunging tank top. A fan of tattooed feathers covers the rise of her breasts. On each feather is a human eye. I try not to stare, but it is an impressive work of art. "What time was it when you left, Grady?"

"Maybe four forty-five or so. Why?"

"Because that means, if she was still intending to get her hair cut, the hair salon was nearby, near enough to reach by bike in fifteen minutes."

"But she didn't have her bike on Friday," I say.

"Well, it was close enough to walk then." Tattoo Girl points a finger at Nikki, but Nikki is already searching beauty salons in the vicinity of the pool.

"Hair 4 U," she reads, "four blocks east."

We change direction and in a matter of minutes, a neon sign looms above us. The smell of hairspray is overpowering. "I can't go in there," Tattoo Girl says, covering her mouth and nose.

Nikki and I approach the blue-haired girl at the desk. Thick metal hoops dangle from her earlobes to her shoulders. Nikki asks and the girl checks the online appointment book. "Nope, nobody did a Catherine Friday evening." She squints at the screen. "Hang on. I'll ask Randy." Stepping behind the partial walls, she taps a tall, lean hairdresser holding a blow-dryer on his shoulder. Randy saunters to the front while I pull up the photo of Catherine and Walter on my phone.

"Never seen her before," he says, "but I did have a no-show Friday." He turns the computer screen so we can see a blank appointment slot at 5 p.m., then grabs a notepad and flips backwards. "Here we go," he says stabbing at a scrawl on the paper. "Catherine. She booked in on Wednesday but didn't show up on Friday. Didn't even call to cancel."

That doesn't seem like a Catherine thing to do. We thank him and head back to the community centre. "So, she decided not to go last minute," I state, but it sounds more like a question.

"Or she couldn't," says Nikki, "for some reason."

"Maybe she just wanted Reg to think that she was going to that party," I say finally.

"Why?" Free Throw is genuinely perplexed.

That's the question! The question without an answer. Even Nikki doesn't have one. "Scott claims he invited her, but she never showed," Nikki adds.

"He may be lying." Tattoo Girl's voice is edgy.

"If Scott is lying and she attended the party, surely someone else would have seen her. If Reg is lying, then perhaps Catherine had no intention of going to the party after all," says Nikki. She pauses, then adds, "And if Catherine's lying, then none of this makes sense."

We have reached a crossroads and stand around impatiently, waiting for the signal to change. My thoughts ricochet around my skull but fail to come to any logical conclusion.

"Look," says Tattoo Girl before the signal flashes, "why don't Free Throw and I head to Scott's, and Grady and Nikki, you guys go use your heads and figure out other potential scenarios. Grady, send me that photo you took of Catherine with the dog. You've got a key to Mrs. Stafford's — we'll meet you there. And make sure Walter has food. Labs don't do well when they're starving."

I am reluctant to use the house, but I did promise Reg I'd check up on the place, so we agree. I take Penny's leash from Free Throw and for a few blocks, I am thrilled at the prospect of walking a real live dog. Penny is excited; she knows she is headed home. The wind is picking up and I'm glad I've worn my hoodie. Nikki and I quicken our pace, and soon I am unlocking the front door of Mrs. Stafford's home. Penny heads for her water dish and Walter barks from the yard. I check that his automatic feeder is still full, then add a scoop of kibble to his bowl anyway and invite him inside.

We sit in the family room, surrounded by pictures of Mrs. Stafford's late daughter, Adrianna. "She was cute," I say.

But Nikki is lost in thought, her fingers punching keys on her phone. "What are you doing?" I ask.

"Trying to figure out why the police are holding Reg."

"Because they're thinking of charging him with abduction," I say. Nikki makes no response. "Because he was the last person to see Catherine, and . . ." I stop there.

She keeps typing, her forehead furrowed, her eyes darting in all directions. Suddenly her face lights up. "I'm in," she says.

Do I dare ask? "In where?"

"It's better if you don't know."

"Don't, Nikki," I protest, "you've already been caught once." I know it isn't that she hasn't considered the repercussions of her actions or that she's disregarded them — she's too logical a sort to ignore all that. She's just made a choice.

"This is," she tells me, "not the time for a philosophical debate, especially one that deals with the subjective interpretation of right and wrong. Besides, the police channels are totally accessible to the public, or at least some of them are." She looks up at me with frank, honest eyes. "If Reg is innocent, he deserves to be free," she says. "Besides, we need to know where Catherine is."

I say nothing. Instead, I examine the pictures of Adrianna throughout the years. Her wide eyes have a whimsical quality to them. Five minutes later, Nikki lays her phone on the couch. "Nothing. I ran Reg's name on a criminal search but obtained no results."

"That's good," I say, "but didn't Tattoo Girl say he did time?"

"Yes," she murmurs. "He was imprisoned in the States, and there are a lot of different databases, but I'm sure he said he was from California. Unless he uses an alias." She searches the room. "I need a photo of Reg."

Tentatively, feeling as if I am an interloper invading Mrs. Stafford's trust, we begin to search. Both of us avoid the bedroom — it's too intimate a place. There are no pictures beneath magnets on the fridge, no glossy prints strewn on phone desks, only photograph albums carefully numbered and dated. I flip through a recent one but there are no photos of Reg, only photos of Mrs. Stafford and miscellaneous smiling folk whom I presume to be relatives. And there are quite a few photos of Mrs. Stafford at receptions, shaking hands with men in suits, presenting cheques to the Canadian Diabetes Association and the Canadian Cancer Society. I slide the album back on its shelf. I am reluctant to look through the others.

Nikki is listening to the police chatting about the upcoming football game, flipping channels, dancing in and out of static. We wait, seated on Mrs. Stafford's leather couch with Penny asleep between us and Walter curled up at our feet. Adrianna's eyes watch us from grinning faces. "She really was cute," I say again, unable to resist the sincerity of the little blond girl who apparently used to ride a three-wheeler, whistle and stomp in the mud. But I am drawn most to a picture of Adrianna when she is about the same age as my little sister. It is a close-up and in it, she sits with her chin on her hands, gazing straight ahead as if preoccupied with — with what I wonder? Birthday parties, new sneakers, cookie dough. "I wonder what complications she died of?" I've said it aloud without meaning to and Nikki, who still does not understand the meaning of a rhetorical question, is already searching for the answer.

"She died on October twenty-seventh in San Diego," Nikki reports. Her voice lowers. "After slipping into a diabetic coma . . ."

I wonder how that happened under Mrs. Stafford's watch. Or if that's the reason she's so keen to promote diabetes education now.

"After being abducted."

I freeze. This is all a bit weird. Nikki revs into action, her lips in constant motion, reading aloud. "She was taken . . . while waiting for the school bus . . . Howard Torrance, a mechanic . . . held for eleven hours . . . Mr. Torrance having lost his own wife and daughter in a car accident weeks earlier."

"He wouldn't have known about her insulin and glucose levels," I hear myself saying. I've learned a lot about diabetes in the past week.

I know what it's like to lose a parent, but I've never thought about what it's like for a parent to lose a child. That's not the natural order of things. I check on the dogs, refill their water dish, then wander into the kitchen and pick up two apples from Mrs. Stafford's fruit bowl. Nikki, as usual, is on her phone when I return to the living room. "Want a Gala apple?" I ask her, winking.

But she does not respond. Her body is tense and poised and the intensity in her eyes is frightening. "Give it a break," I say. "The others should be back soon." I turn back towards the kitchen, but her voice summons me.

"Grady, come here." It is not a request.

I retrace my footsteps and peer over Nikki's shoulder at a photograph of a man with a moustache and beard. He is heavy set with chubby cheeks, pudgy ears and longish hair. "Who's that?" I ask her.

"The guy who abducted Adrianna. The one who didn't know she had diabetes."

As I watch, she begins to alter his features. First, the moustache and beard go, then the chubbiness around the cheeks, then the hair gets cut short.

"Reg!" My whisper is a gunshot in the night. I sink to the floor beside her. "That's why they are holding him."

Nikki's head nods as I process this new information. Reg kidnapped Adrianna and let her die. Our Reg killed a little girl. "Do you think he abducted Catherine?" I ask, my mouth pasty with thick saliva.

But before she can speculate, the doorbell announces Free Throw and Tattoo Girl.

"Let's keep this to ourselves for now," I whisper as I head to the front door to let them in.

Luckily neither seems to notice my angst. Tattoo Girl helps herself to a beer in the fridge. She sets three other cold ones down on the coffee table and sinks into the couch. "Go on," she says. Free Throw shakes his head, and I wonder if he's abstaining because of his dad. Nikki passes. I reach for one and open the pull tab, but I don't drink.

In a calm voice, Tattoo Girl tells us what they didn't find at Scott's.

Scott's place is a large, gated brick house with a manicured lawn out front. It sits at the end of a cul-de-sac, a sprawling mansion according to Free Throw that could house his entire extended family. When Tattoo Girl and Free Throw approached the house, they were informed by the gardener that Master Killick was in the pool. He led them around back, and Scott was more than a little surprised to see them. He's had no word from Catherine.

Tattoo Girl continues. "Scott admits to having invited her to the party but claims she didn't come. Guests started arriving around five p.m. for the barbeque he'd organized, but he was adamant that the last time he saw Catherine was at the pool. Besides, he made sure we knew he was completely preoccupied with Bridget on Friday evening." At this point in the story, Tattoo Girl sticks a finger in her open mouth and makes a surprisingly realistic gagging sound.

"So, we still don't know if Reg is lying or not," I say dismally.

"Correct," says Tattoo Girl. She takes a long swig of her beer. I reach for the cold can and place it against my forehead.

# CHAPTER 11

Nikki has her earbuds stuck in her ears. She pulls them out now and tells us that the police are under pressure to open a missing persons file on Catherine, but that they'll likely wait until the full twenty-four hours before doing so. It's standard police protocol. "Then they'll be wanting to interview us."

We look at each other and wonder what we will tell them? I think about the last time I saw Catherine at the pool. She was carrying her purple handbag and her backpack, and her eyes were blue. And now, she's missing. "Let's go over what we know so far, again," I say with a quiver in my voice.

We take turns listing details. She bought new clothes and contacts last week. Her grandmother died. She didn't ride her bike to work on Friday like she usually does. She told Reg she was going to Scott's party, but apparently didn't go. Nor did she go to her hair appointment. Her glasses were found in the parking lot outside Reg's apartment. She's not answering her cell phone, and she's disappeared.

"And she had her backpack with her Friday," I add, sensing that I've missed something.

"Her backpack?" says Tattoo Girl, scowling. "You're sure? I've never seen her carry a backpack, just that ridiculous lilac handbag."

"I'm sure!"

Free Throw returns to the question that continues to plague us. "So why ask Reg to drop her at Scott's if she didn't want to go to his party?"

Tattoo Girl stands, her eyes shimmering. "Because she wanted it to seem like she'd gone to Scott's," she says, "so nobody would know that she'd run away."

Like frames of a film, I see Catherine sitting at the concession booth, alone. I recall the way she recoiled when Tattoo Girl first threatened her, the way she fawned over Scott during the pool cleanout, her brittle words when she told us her grandmother had died, her angst when she saw Scott and Bridget. It's possible she ran away. I feel a pang of guilt for not making an effort, for not trying to include her. Then again, who'd want to be a part of the Nothing Club? Now I wonder why I'm trying to find her. To save Reg or because she might be in trouble? I sense it's both. "Okay, so where would she go and how did she get there?"

Penny digs a ball out from under the couch and noses it onto a cushion. She backs up and barks to get Free Throw's attention. Even Walter raises his massive head and looks like he might want to play, but nobody engages. We are all focused on the question at hand.

Nikki leans back against the couch. "I sorted through all her social media posts but found nothing helpful."

"Catherine has a big online presence?" I ask, surprised. My mom isn't a big fan of social media, so I have none.

"Surprisingly so," says Nikki, "although there's not much that's personal on it."

"Smart girl," mutters Tattoo Girl. I am shocked by her

comment. I glance at Free Throw, then realize for the first time that the guy doesn't have his own cell phone. Wow!

"Numerous posts about natural remedies," adds Nikki. "And a plethora of animal photos, especially llamas."

I recall our conversation about her wanting to get a llama. She'd need a farm for that. "Wait a minute. I've got it!" I make eye contact with the others. "She's gone to her grandparents' farm! The one with the hayloft fort."

It's as good a guess as any, and in minutes Nikki has pulled up Catherine's grandmother's funeral announcement, located the farm and has a Google Map on her screen directing us to Mason Anderson's house 56 kilometres outside of the city, near the town of Ridgeview. "Let's go!" calls Free Throw.

We jump to our feet, then look sheepishly at each other. "A bus?" I suggest. A quick check reveals the next one leaves tomorrow morning, but there was one out at 6:30 p.m. on Friday.

"That doesn't mean that she was on that bus," says Nikki purposefully. "And it would hardly be prudent to embark on some wild chase to Ridgeview without ascertaining that Catherine actually went there."

"The only way we can know is to go find her," I say, exasperation creeping into my voice.

"Not necessarily," says Nikki, zeroing in on her phone screen. "Bus stations have video surveillance and . . ." I'm pretty sure that video surveillance footage from the public bus station is not accessible to the public, but I move so that I can look over her shoulder anyway.

"Stop!" I cry as she scrolls through footage from Friday night. "That purse. Do you see that purple handbag?" All we can see is a glimpse of a lilac purse over a bench, but it is enough. We jump into action.

Tattoo Girl disappears and I hear a door creak open. "Does anybody drive?" she asks. We join her at the door leading into the garage where Mrs. Stafford's black Audi sits, glistening in the dim light.

Although Free Throw and Tattoo Girl are both fifteen like me, I am the only one with my learner's. "I've only ever driven my mom's old beater," I protest, as Tattoo Girl hands me the car keys and Nikki climbs into the passenger seat. Reluctantly, I get behind the wheel. There is no point in arguing. We have to get to Ridgeview and, as wild as it sounds, this makes the most sense. We leave Walter behind, ensure his dog door is open and his feeder full and take Penny.

Rich tan leather cradles my shoulders and hips. I open the garage door, adjust my seat and the rearview mirror as Tattoo Girl and Free Throw belt up in the back seat. Penny perches on a blanket between them. The engine purrs to life. I gingerly shift into reverse. Thankfully the car is in a double garage, and I don't have to navigate out of a tight space. Soon, miraculously, we are backing out of the driveway. My hands clutch the steering wheel so tightly that my wrists hurt, but gradually I relax them, wriggle my pinky fingers and let my elbows drop. I shift into drive, and we creep forward. We've only gone about ten blocks when the gas light comes on. "Damn!" I pull over and dig out my wallet. $2.35. Tattoo Girl is broke, and Nikki has a toonie in her pocket.

I have cash on my desk at home, but if I go home driving an Audi my mother will flip, and I don't have my bank card.

"Take your third left." Tattoo Girl directs me with inked fingers. "I know where I can get some cash."

Something in her voice makes me chomp down hard on the obvious question, but I follow her directions. She points at a rundown brick house with a windowless white door, and I pull up in front of it. "Keep the engine running," she says, slamming the car door behind her. She disappears around the side, and I leave the car idling. Free Throw and Nikki watch anxiously, and Penny presses her nose against the glass. In just a few moments, the three of us are breathing in unison. Inhaling trepidation, exhaling hope. Sixty-eight breaths later, the front door opens, and Tattoo Girl struts out onto the porch, tugging the door closed behind her. I half-expect her to sprint to the car, so I flex my ankle, ready to accelerate away from whatever danger lurks within. But instead, she stands, uncaps a black felt pen and begins to draw on the door.

"What's she doing?" asks Nikki in disbelief.

"Tattooing the door," replies Free Throw.

I recognize the tattoo the moment she steps aside — an antelope taking down a lion. And suddenly I know that this place belongs to Rigoh, the lion in her life. But now the antelope has usurped the lion. What, I wonder, will the lion do in retaliation? She is hardly in the car when I pull away from the curb.

She leans over the front seat and drops a wad of cash between me and Nikki. "Here," she says. "Gas money."

Just then I catch sight of a guy in a rust-coloured jacket weaving down the sidewalk. I'm just thinking that I know him from somewhere when Free Throw pipes up. "Hey, that's Billy. Stop the car." I step on the brake as a black pickup turns onto the street and rolls towards me.

"No!" commands Tattoo Girl. "Let's go!" Rigoh is behind the wheel of the truck, Bald Guy in the passenger seat.

"Get down!" I order and everyone including me ducks. The Audi veers too far to the right and we bump against the curb. Rigoh rolls down the street, with only a disdainful glance at me, then stops beside Billy. I slip past him, step on the gas and turn left heading towards the highway.

"What was Billy doing there?" asks Free Throw.

"Rigoh's his dealer," says Tattoo Girl, without much emotion. It's just a fact, a fact that Free Throw doesn't seem to want to register.

I imagine Rigoh rolling to a stop beside Billy, then driving home, seeing the house door, making a connection to seeing me at the Sugar Shack, Bald Guy smashing the door open, Rigoh finding the cash missing and leaping back into the truck. The gas light blinks again, and I turn into a gas station and fill up. How long will it take the lion to put the pieces together?

Finally, when the tank is full, I ease back onto the highway but keep my eyes flickering from the rearview mirror to the side mirror to the road ahead. No sign of a black pickup so far. Maybe they took Billy home. Whenever a vehicle approaches, I find myself hoping it's not Rigoh or a cop. I wonder which would be better. Rigoh might run us off the road, but the cop would arrest four juveniles in community service in a borrowed car who might have information about an abduction, with a wad of money that came from ... where did it come from?

"Is there a phone charging cord in the glovebox?" asks Tattoo Girl. Nikki checks the glovebox but finds only the owner's manual and car registration. At least I know where that is if I need it.

Tattoo Girl tucks her phone in her pocket and leans back against the headrest. As we drive, I steal a glance at her in my rearview mirror. She's mentioned a drug deal, she's been battered by Rigoh, she calls them family, she knows Free Throw's druggie brother and she's the official word on the streets, but what hold do they have on her?

We drive through a treed area and Free Throw snores softly in the back seat. Tattoo Girl, unaware that I am watching her, relaxes. She brushes her hair back from her eyes and gazes out the window, lost in thought. Her lips part in a smile and her energy softens.

"You like the country?" I ask her.

"I used to," she says. An ambulance screams past us. In the rearview mirror, I see that raindrops have collected in the corner of Tattoo Girl's eyes.

It is after three by the time Nikki directs me onto a side road just before we reach Ridgeview, and my stomach growls. The entire drive, 56 kilometres, has taken an hour and fifty minutes. Nobody has said a derogatory word, and I am as grateful to them for that as I am for Tattoo Girl's strong hands massaging my neck.

"Let's go into town," I suggest, "and see what we can find out about the grandparents."

"Just like the movies," says Free Throw.

We stop at a Dairy Queen, and I order four burgers and fries for everyone. When I slip Tattoo Girl's money onto the counter, I wonder if it's counterfeit, but the cashier doesn't seem concerned. Nikki has never had a fast-food burger and only manages to stomach half, before sliding it towards Free Throw. He wraps it up for Penny, who is waiting in the car. We bide our time, looking for the right informants.

Halfway through my dill pickle, an older couple sits down beside us to enjoy their strawberry sundaes. "Excuse me," I say, crossing towards their table. "We're looking for Mason Anderson's farm. Would you be able to tell us where that is?"

The woman wipes her hands on her napkin. "Mason's place, well of course, everyone knows Mason's place. It's the big old farmhouse just east of the 247 on Range Road 63." Her smile fades. "But he's been gone for years and well, his widow just passed too."

"Oh," I say looking crestfallen and trying to sound older

than I am. "Mason's a distant relative. My dad spent time on that farm, and I was hoping to see it."

The man offers a bit of advice. "The place is rented to a Robert Hoffman. A few people from the city board horses with him, but he's a rather surly sort. Keeps to himself mostly. I know he's got two Dobermans as guard dogs, and they don't take kindly to visitors."

I gulp. That is where we are headed.

"There aren't many landmarks out that way," the man adds. "You turn left at the junction of the two roads, then it's about three kilometres down the 63 to the driveway. If you pass Ann and Harvey's little white bungalow, you've gone too far."

"You can always stop at Ann's for directions," his wife says, then corrects herself. "Except they are away at their niece's wedding this weekend."

"I'm sure we'll be able to find it. Thank you," I say. We clear our garbage and get up to go. The sun is off its high axis. "The farm?" I ask as we approach the car.

"Nope, the grocery store," says Free Throw, "to buy a couple of marrow bones. No dog can resist a marrow bone."

While he purchases the bones, Tattoo Girl buys a phone charger and plugs it into the Audi's charging port. Her phone beeps to life.

The marrow bones reek in the back seat, although Free Throw doesn't seem to notice. Penny does, but Free Throw offers her the rest of Nikki's burger instead. Nikki is scheming on her phone and Tattoo Girl is lost in thought again. Driving Mrs. Stafford's expensive vehicle down a rough gravel road, I can almost hear the rocks chipping the paint. I try not to think about that as I turn onto the 63 and park in a roadside pullout not far from the entrance to the farm. The dogs haven't noticed us yet or at least there's no sign of them.

"Grady, I'm staying here," says Nikki. "Well, actually there." She points up a tall willow tree as we stare at her with blank looks on our faces. "With this," she adds, pressing the play button on her phone. Penny erupts into a barking fit. Tattoo Girl covers her ears and moans, but Free Throw and I hear nothing. "It's a high-pitched dog whistle." Nikki grins. "I downloaded it awhile back when Reg mentioned it." And suddenly I am reminded of that conversation so many days ago — the one about sensing without the senses. "Those Dobermans will hear it and hopefully run in my direction. That will give you time to get down the driveway and assess the situation. And last time I researched, Dobermans don't climb." She looks a little nervous, but I admire her bravery and ingenuity.

She climbs out of the car and Free Throw boosts her onto a branch, then directs her upwards. Soon she is barely visible, her back solidly against a Y in the trunk of the tree about five metres off the ground. "Stay safe, Nikki Wiki," he calls as Tattoo Girl climbs into the front seat beside me.

I inch the car along the road and turn onto the gravel driveway. My heartbeat accelerates as I step on the gas. I roll along looking for the Dobermans but they are nowhere in sight. Nikki's whistle must be working. The house is a run-down old farmhouse that must have once been quite elegant. It is a full two storeys with a steep attic and shutters on the windows. A long verandah wraps around the front of the house overlooking a fenced pasture where three horses graze. Tattoo Girl mutters, "What a beautiful animal," under her breath and points at a fourth horse, a sleek paint mare with white patches, in a paddock.

I notice that the front door had, at some point, been painted a striking teal colour, although it is faded now. But the driveway doesn't lead to the front door. Rather it curves around the back of the house. We follow it and just as the rear of the house becomes visible, spot a set of stairs clinging to the corner of the home. A well-used wooden porch runs almost the full length of the rear of the house. The window shutters half-hang from their hinges, battered by the winds and forgotten by the owners. I turn and park beside a shed that lists slightly to the right.

A man's face appears at the window of the house. "Free Throw, you stay here," I instruct, "and keep Penny quiet."

Free Throw cradles the dog in his arms and slides his long spine down the rear seat until he is almost horizontal.

Tattoo Girl and I get out and approach the back door. It swings open as we arrive and a whiskered man marches onto the porch. He puts two grimy fingers in his mouth and whistles, but the dogs are gone. "You're trespassing," he growls.

"We're looking for Mason Anderson," I say trying to quell the tremble in my voice. "He's a relative of my father's."

"Dead," says the man and I catch a glimpse of broken, nicotine-stained teeth. Thin hair covers his balding head and his eyes squint when he gazes in my direction. But mostly, he watches Tattoo Girl, drinking her in. She acts as if she is oblivious to his presence, but runs her fingers through her dark hair, arching her back seductively to reach the ends that cascade between her shoulder blades. Then she turns and deliberately meets his eyes.

"Are you a relative?" I ask him, glancing at Tattoo Girl and wondering what the hell has gotten into her. She holds his gaze steadily.

He looks back in my direction. "No, a tenant. Now get off the property."

Suddenly, Tattoo Girl is on the first wooden step leading to the porch. She grabs the rail and swings upward, placing one lace-up black boot solidly on the worn wood, then looking up at Hoffman again. "Hey," she says with a provocative indifference.

Hoffman doesn't reply but I swear he drools. Tattoo Girl steps up another stair. "Would you mind if I used your bathroom? Been in the car a long time." Without waiting for an answer, she sidles past him, her breasts almost brushing his chest.

He follows Tattoo Girl into the house, and I tag along after him, through an oil-stained kitchen to a dusty living room where Tattoo Girl appears to be searching for the bathroom.

"There," Hoffman says, pointing to a small room off the kitchen. He positions himself at the base of the stairs and watches as she disappears inside. Tinny country music emanates from an old transistor radio.

I take the opportunity to check the place out — but I can't see much from the back door, except for the kitchen. It is filthy and, after working in the doughnut shop all summer, makes me appreciate health regulations. A shotgun leans against the door frame just inside the kitchen door. I gulp. "I'll just wait on the porch," I tell Hoffman and return the way I came in. Tattoo Girl takes her time, giving me a chance to survey the area.

To my right, at the far end of the porch sits a large wire enclosure with two doghouses and numerous half-chewed bones inside. Three hundred metres beyond that is a sturdy rectangular barn, oriented perpendicular to the farmhouse. It is the classic red wooden barn with a two-slope design roof made of shiny new metal. I can just make out the outline of the hayloft door high on the narrow end nearest me; the barn's main door must be on the far end. There is a berm on the far side of the barn bordered by a dense hedge of shrubs and a wooded area in the distance. Closer to the house, a few hundred metres away, is an overgrown garden and next to it, the shed I parked beside. When Tattoo Girl reappears, I hustle her down the stairs towards the Audi. That's when we notice that Free Throw and Penny aren't in the back seat. "Shit," I whisper.

Tattoo Girl opens the rear passenger door then peels off her jean jacket, revealing her fan of feathery eyes. She tosses the jacket onto the seat, pivots on the heel of her boot and saunters back towards the house. "Is there a gas station nearby?" she asks sweetly.

"A mile south of here." I can almost hear Hoffman salivate.

She turns in a graceful circle at the bottom of the steps as I search frantically for Free Throw. He motions at me from the front bumper, and I jerk my head to the left, indicating that the car door is open.

Tattoo Girl sees him too. Her giggle doesn't belong to her. "I'm so hopeless with directions," she tells Hoffman strutting towards him until she is directly on the stair in front of him. She gestures helplessly, palms up. "And where exactly would that be?"

Hoffman raises one finger and points down the driveway, drawing directions in the air as Free Throw ducks into the car.

"Let's go," I call and Tattoo Girl pivots again, sashaying across the dusty farmyard.

"Thanks so much, Robert." she pauses, then adds, "It is Robert, isn't it?" Hoffman looks momentarily surprised, then grunts and nods. "It must be lonely living out here on your own." She smiles seductively at him, and I throw her a scornful look before ducking into the driver's seat. Free Throw is flattened against the back seat, holding Penny. I rev the engine to life as Tattoo Girl takes her time getting in. She lowers the window and waves as we pull out, then discreetly snaps a few photos of the farmhouse while we cruise down the driveway.

"What was that all about?" I bark as we reach the road. She sets her lips tightly together. "Just in case."

"In case what?" Anger edges upwards. I want to shake her, but I'm driving. I glance down at my cell phone. It is a few minutes before five. Almost exactly twenty-four hours since Catherine went missing.

When we reach the road, we make a beeline for Nikki. The dogs are at the base of the tree and even Free Throw isn't too keen to get out. Instead, he opens the sunroof, throws one marrow bone in the direction of the Dobermans and instructs Nikki to hang from a limb above the car. She does and with ease, Free Throw reaches up and grabs her legs, hauling her in through the sunroof. Her laughter fills the air, and I realize it is the first time I have heard her laugh. We speed down the road with the dogs chasing behind us.

## CHAPTER 12

Evening is upon us when we finally stop at a gas station just outside Ridgeview. My body feels tense and my shoulder muscles ache, but I get out, go in, and buy cold drinks and bags of chips for all of us. We sit in the car sipping our drinks and updating one another.

Free Throw goes first. "I made it to the barn," he says, "but the whole thing is padlocked shut. And the ground-floor windows have been boarded up. Like he's got something to hide."

"It is unlikely that Catherine would have reached the barn with those dogs guarding the premises," Nikki tells us. "They are killers, both of them."

"Hoffman stayed at the bottom of the stairs," I add.

"Mmm," says Tattoo Girl softly, her head leaning against the passenger side window across the seat from me. "Catherine's on the second floor."

Nikki leans forward. "You saw her or saw some indication of her presence?"

Tattoo Girl shakes her head. "No, but I know. She's there."

Nikki sighs in partial disbelief and partial frustration. Tattoo Girl doesn't respond. We are no further ahead than we were, but I remind myself, that we are no further behind either. Or at least I don't think so until Rigoh's black pickup rolls into the gas station lot.

"Go!" cries Tattoo Girl. I step on the gas and tear out of the station, but it is too late. He's spotted us and the chase is on, although we have a bit of a lead because he has to get past the pumps first and there are a few vehicles coming and going. "Faster," screams Tattoo Girl as I zigzag around a median and lay rubber onto a rural grid road. Reg would kill me if he saw me driving like this. A pang of guilt hits me in the chest and I slow down.

"Remember we're doing this for Reg," declares Tattoo Girl as if she's read my mind. I floor it, then turn right, left, a sharp right and hit the brakes behind a semi-trailer parked in a road stop. Rigoh zooms by.

"Good thing this car has good pick up," says Free Throw, gripping my headrest.

My heart hammers above the roar of the engine. "Okay, what's the plan?" I ask Nikki as we watch the tail lights disappear on the horizon.

"To find Catherine and exonerate Reg," she states flatly.

"And exactly how are we going to do that?" asks Tattoo Girl with more than a hint of irritation in her voice.

"That depends on whether Catherine is at the farm or not," Nikki says matter-of-factly. "That must be our first discovery."

She seems oblivious to the fact that Rigoh and Bald Guy, probably armed and dangerous, are searching for Tattoo Girl and the money. Or that the police are likely trying to track us down for questioning right now. My phone is dead. I plug it in and notice the fifteen text messages from my mother. That's when I also realize that my forehead is beaded with sweat. What the hell are we doing here?

Before we can think, Rigoh's black pickup rolls past us and the parked semi. I hit the gas and screech out onto the secondary highway in the opposite direction, but Rigoh pulls a U-turn and roars after me. Suddenly the scream of sirens fills the air behind us. Blue and red lights flash behind Rigoh's truck as I ease off the gas and keep driving, incredibly thankful that they can only pull one of us over. Once Rigoh's truck is out of sight, I turn into town, determined to lose our tail.

"How did he know to come back for us?" Tattoo Girl asks. Her voice shimmies up and down.

"He must have seen you pull off," says Free Throw.

"No, he went by us, and then all of a sudden, there he was," I say. Something doesn't compute.

Tattoo Girl is perspiring, giving her tattoos an inky sheen. "It's always that way," she groans. "No matter where I go, he can find me."

Nikki extends one hand over the headrest. "Cell phone," she mutters, and Tattoo Girl hands over her phone. "He's tracking you," she says.

Tattoo Girl curses. "It's no wonder he bought me this fancy phone," she murmurs, "and even set it up for me. What a gentleman."

Nikki confidently presses and swipes Tattoo Girl's phone. Her eyes are thoughtful. "Find My Device could conceivably enable us to track Catherine even if her phone is off —" begins Nikki.

"Really?" I interrupt.

"If we had access to her personal information." Nikki returns the phone to Tattoo Girl. "I disabled that feature," she explains. "In this case, it is not especially beneficial."

"We have to go back. I know she's there." Tattoo Girl's eyes are closed. I wonder how she can be so sure. "Upstairs," she adds, and I find myself agreeing although I wish I didn't.

Nikki dismisses her. "Unless you saw some sign of Catherine or some object that she had in her possession, then there —"

"When I know, I know," snaps Tattoo Girl.

Free Throw and I sit in silence as Nikki struggles with this declaration. There isn't a shred of evidence we can offer her and yet, I too suspect that Tattoo Girl is correct.

"What you are claiming," Nikki finally states, "is that you practise claircognizance. Do you also indulge in clairaudience and clairalience?" It is part rhetorical question, part statement and part accusation. I make a mental note to look up those "clairs" if I can remember them. I glance at Tattoo Girl, trying to ascertain if she knows what Nikki's talking about, but her face divulges nothing.

Instead, Tattoo Girl's resolute eyes meet Nikki's. "What I'm telling you is that she's there. I know down here." Her hands cover her gut.

"Great," says Nikki, lifting her palms in a surrendering gesture. "We are going to make strategic, potentially life-threatening plans based on Tattoo Girl's large intestine." Nobody disagrees. "Okay, did anyone see an upstairs window?"

"Yeah, but they're boarded up." Free Throw sounds worried. Even his happy simplicity can't weather this.

"I thought there was glass," I say.

"Boarded," insists Free Throw as Penny settles into his lap.

Nikki checks Google Earth. The windows out front are partially boarded up just as Free Throw thought. "But there's no way of knowing if this is a recent photo or about the windows on the back side," she explains.

"Which is why I took these," says Tattoo Girl pulling up the pictures she snapped from the driveway. Nikki zooms in. There is glass on the upper windows. Her slender fingers point to the strange set of stairs we noticed on the way in.

"Look! There's an old external fire exit staircase descending from the top floor." So that's what that is. Nikki lays out her plan in a single sentence. "We need to return to Hoffman's place, create a distraction for the dogs in order to facilitate the climbing of a fire escape that hopefully leads to a second-storey room where Catherine may be being held."

It sounds so easy, so logical, even mundane, and yet I know it's ludicrous. I pull into a school playground and park where I have easy access to the exit.

"Given the present condition of the home," she continues, "it is doubtful that the window will open, so whoever climbs to her rescue will also likely have to find a way to get through that window and extricate Catherine, preferably without inflicting damage on themselves, and without attracting the attention of Hoffman."

I contemplate dislodging a window. "I can do that," I say, attempting to sound confident.

"No," says Tattoo Girl. "You're the driver. The driver always stays with the vehicle." She says it with an authority that is unquestionable.

"Then let me go," say Free Throw and Nikki simultaneously.

"Nikki Wiki, you're more valuable for your brains than your muscle," declares Tattoo Girl. "Besides, we're going to need some more high-pitched dog calls."

"Good," says Free Throw. There is no hesitation in his voice.

Tattoo Girl nods. "Okay, so here's the plan. When it's almost dark, we go in again, leave Nikki at the tree, wait for the dogs to respond to her whistle, drive in and park like we did last time. Then I'll get out of the car, as if I've driven in alone, and distract Hoffman. Grady stays low in the driver's seat, and Free Throw, you get around the car to the edge of the house and over to the fire escape." She pauses. "Once you and Catherine are back in the car, Grady, you lay on the horn and point the nose of the car down the lane. Free Throw, make sure the back door of the car is open. Pick me up and we're outta there."

I stare at Tattoo Girl with wide eyes. "You're kidding, right?" I ask, although somehow I don't think she is.

"That plan is impractical," agrees Nikki. "It may take Free Throw some time to access the stairs and force entry, then descend with Catherine. If she's hurt or unconscious, that duration could be up to twenty minutes. That's too long for a distraction."

Tattoo Girl laughs, an ugly, bitter laugh. "Twenty minutes is nothing," she says. "Trust me."

Suddenly I know what she's going to do. "No!" I say.

Tattoo Girl crosses her arms and gives me a half-open-eyed look. "You got a better idea?" she challenges.

I rack my brains but come up with nothing.

She softens. "Look, Grady, it's not like I've never done this before, you know. It'll be okay. I know these guys." She blushes as we all protest, then holds up one hand. The lovebirds on her palm hover as if still connected to the rose bush on the inside of her forearm. Then her fingers relax, and the birds take flight. "Before I met Rigoh, I lived on the streets," she says finally, and her words are heavy with resignation. "You do what you have to do to survive. I can keep Hoffman there for twenty minutes easy."

Free Throw's eyes grow shiny. Nikki's already pale face drains until she resembles a ghost.

"No way," I say softly. "It's not worth it. We're not asking you to do that."

"Catherine's not worth it?" Tattoo Girl asks. I swallow the lump in my throat but say nothing. "She has parents, a brother, cats. I'm . . . I'm nothing like that." Like the birds on her palm, her words flutter around the car, suspended above the leather seats looking for a place to settle, begging for a home.

Nikki is the first to offer them a place to roost. She puts a hand on Tattoo Girl's shoulder. "There are few friends who would make such a sacrifice," she says quietly. Free Throw clamps a huge hand over Nikki's.

They all look at me.

Tattoo Girl touches my forearm. "It's okay," she says softly, and I slip my hand over Free Throw's. The lovebirds cover my knuckles in solidarity. "Now, what time is sunset?"

Nikki checks her phone. "Nine thirty-seven."

Just then our screens scream simultaneously. It's an amber alert for Catherine.

We pass the time at the school playground, keeping a sharp eye out for Rigoh and Bald Guy and the cops. I hope that the cops searched the truck, found drugs and hauled them into the station, but my gut tells me they probably just got a speeding ticket. My mom calls for the seventeenth time, but I don't pick up. What would I tell her?

While we wait, we play on the monkey bars and curly slides, like overgrown innocent children. Tattoo Girl climbs onto the swing and Free Throw pushes her while Penny chases her tail and barks. Tattoo Girl soars into the air, her hair standing straight out at the pinnacle of her arc. Then suddenly, she grips the chains, throws her head backwards and plummets towards the ground leaning backwards out of the swing. "My gut," she moans, pulling herself back into a sitting position and grabbing her stomach. I sprint to the swing beside her, pump myself into the air, then pull the chains outwards at the top of my arc. They slam together hitting my head. "Your head!" she cries, laughing.

Where did we learn to swing? I wonder. And why do we

tempt fate even in play? "What makes a risk taker?" I ask as I scuff my shoes in the gravel below me.

"Passion," replies Nikki. "Being afraid that you will die without having done something amazing to benefit mankind." Her life in a nutshell!

"Desperation," says Free Throw. "When there's no way out of a bad situation, people take risks." I think of his brother and wonder if his risks ever involve Free Throw.

"Guilt." Tattoo Girl's voice rises on the wind as she swings above us. But she doesn't add anything, and we don't ask.

I deliberate for a moment. Why did I take the risk I did with the fireworks? Was it all for the thrill of the moment? "Stupidity," I say finally. "And not wanting to look like a wuss." I scoop Penny up and hold her on my lap.

Tattoo Girl gives me an oblique smile. "You told me you were a wuss the first time I met you," she reminds me.

I chuckle as Free Throw, seated on the see-saw, uses his weight to hold Nikki in the air. "I am," I say. "I don't have an ounce of courage in me."

"Okay," says Tattoo Girl, "but you're having a hard time convincing me today."

Free Throw jolts the seat of the see-saw onto the ground, bouncing Nikki up and down on the other end. She shrieks, then grabs the handle. Soon she is full of contagious giggles. Tattoo Girl twirls in her swing, and I wind my chain as tight as possible, then let it go. Penny's shrill bark fills the air. We spin, wildly smashing our legs against one another's. I catch my breath and watch Nikki climb over the handle of the see-saw and inch her way towards Free Throw on her belly. He pushes upwards and she slides back down, shrieking.

An RCMP car rolls into the parking lot of the school and we freeze. My heartbeat is loud enough to echo off the metal slide, but we clamber off the playground equipment and stand around with deliberate casualness.

"Hey," says the officer, getting out of his vehicle. Penny growls and I hold her muzzle. "We're looking for a girl about your age." He pulls out a photo of Catherine and hands it to Tattoo Girl. It is a portrait picture of her in a school uniform, with her hair in soft waves and her makeup done. I am struck by how pretty she looks. "Any of you know this girl? Her name is Catherine Anderson. She disappeared yesterday in the city."

"Why are you looking for her out here?" asks Tattoo Girl.

My hands are sweaty, and I try not to look too interested. The last thing I need is the officer wanting to see my licence or the car registration.

"Her grandparents had a farm out here."

"Sorry," says Tattoo Girl, "we don't know anybody who looks like that." It is remarkable how she manages to lie while telling the truth. Tattoo Girl hands the photo back to the officer. "Good luck."

The officer glances at the Audi and eyes us suspiciously. "Nice wheels."

My feet sink into the ground, cementing me to the spot. Suddenly, the Mountie's radio crackles, and he hesitates. It crackles again. He reaches through the cruiser's open window, pulls the radio towards his mouth and speaks. Then he jumps into the vehicle, pulling the car door shut behind him. "Call 911 if you see her," he calls as he reverses out of the playground and speeds away.

I let out an enormous sigh of relief and rein in my imagination before it descends into reality. It is almost sunset. We climb back into the Audi and head back towards Catherine's grandparents' place. I find myself wondering why we didn't just tell the RCMP officer about her. Then again, we are four missing kids sentenced to community service, driving a borrowed Audi! "Do you think the RCMP searched the farm?" asks Nikki as the wind bows down the wheat fields next to us.

"Not unless they had a search warrant," answers Tattoo Girl. "And there'd be no reason to get one."

But there is a reason. Catherine may be bound and gagged in an upstairs room while Hoffman . . . I don't go there. Hoffman, I know, will be waiting for us with the shotgun loaded. We keep driving in his direction. Validation that we are truly out of our minds!

## CHAPTER 13

When we reach Nikki's willow I stop. The sun is about to tumble down a slight rise in the distance. Nikki punches a button, Penny barks and Tattoo Girl covers her ears. "Are you all deaf?" she says, wincing.

"Apparently," I tell her.

"There," says Tattoo Girl, "the dogs are coming."

In the distance, I can hear a faint barking if I strain myself. "Okay, Nikki. Up you go." Free Throw positions himself beneath the willow, ready to boost her.

"Wait!" Tattoo Girl tilts her head. "The dogs are no closer." It's true. The barking remains at a distance. A cool breeze fills the vehicle as we wait.

"It sounds like the dogs are restricted somehow," says Tattoo Girl. "Near the house."

"They must be in their kennel," I say. "Now what?"

Free Throw reaches beneath the seat and pulls out the other marrow bone he bought earlier. "Maybe this will come in handy," he says as I restart the engine and everyone climbs back in.

A thousand questions surge through my mind. Will Hoffman let the dogs out? Will Free Throw be able to scale that ancient fire escape? What will Hoffman's reaction be when Tattoo Girl gets out of the car?

"Drive!" says Tattoo Girl and I do because she's the dictator antelope.

I turn into the long driveway and Tattoo Girl sidles towards me on the seat. I let the car roll to a halt. "Okay," she orders, "you two get down in the back." She is practically on top of me. "Now Grady, as we get close to the house, I'm going to take the wheel and sit on your lap. You need to duck and press the pedals, okay? Because I've never driven."

"What?" I sputter, but suddenly she is on top of my lap. I slink down and try to find a place for my hands. Finally, I place them on the leather seats beside Tattoo Girl's thighs. I press my forehead into her jean jacket trying to focus on my feet. We swerve right, then left then right again.

"Easy," she says, "slow down. I need to park." I try to block out the image of the Audi careening into the shed and back off the gas pedal. "I could walk faster than this," she quips as I see the glimmer of the light fixed to a pole in the yard. I give her some gas, and she turns left and parks beside Hoffman's old beater truck.

Hoffman is at the base of the stairs; the kennel door is open and immediately the car is flanked by two growling Dobermans. Tattoo Girl leaps off my lap and out the door, leaving the keys in the ignition. The dogs surround her. "Oh no, Robert, help!" screams Tattoo Girl in a high-pitched squeal that is so unlike her. She slams the car door, protecting me from canine teeth.

Hoffman whistles and the growling recedes. "What are you doing here? And where's your boyfriend?"

I feel the heat in my cheeks. Tattoo Girl's voice moves in his direction. "Oh, he's not my boyfriend," she purrs. "I like a more manly type."

For a moment I am insulted, but I have to admit that I feel anything but manly.

"Why'd you come back?" he growls, but there is more curiosity in his voice now.

"Thought you might like a little company. Maybe we could have a whisky or something." Her voice turns sultry. "Besides, I didn't see a woman around earlier."

I don't hear his response, but his footsteps clump up the stairs followed by Tattoo Girl's softer ones. As soon as the door bangs shut, the dogs return to the car. Free Throw and Nikki creak to life in the back seat.

"Open the sunroof," Free Throw orders. I do and he launches the marrow bone in the direction of the kennel. The dogs race towards it, and Free Throw slips out the door on the opposite side of the car, leaving Penny in the back seat. He races across the yard, but despite his speed, the dogs are on to him. I watch as he leaps onto the third stair of the fire escape. Dogs can climb stairs even if they can't climb trees. Free Throw stumbles and I hear the splinter of wood. Steps give way as he scrambles upward, grappling to hold onto the teetering railing. He draws himself up onto a small remaining platform. The dogs leap towards him but there is only air between them and Free Throw. I snuggle Penny close trying to keep her quiet as the Doberman's barking escalates. Free Throw calls softly to them and they quiet, but it's too late.

"Shut up!" screams Hoffman, coming to the door. He is bare-chested, and I feel sick. Free Throw leans back into the blackness. I shrink down, peering between the headrest extenders through the rear window.

Tattoo Girl's face appears behind Hoffman. We can't hear what she says, but she strokes his bare back, enticing him to come back inside.

"I said shut up!" The dogs fall silent at the corner of the house. Hoffman can't see the fire escape from where he is on the porch, but I wonder if he'll be suspicious enough to check it out. Tattoo Girl tugs at his belt. He curses, grabs her by the arm and shoves her inside.

Nikki slips between the seats into the front passenger seat. She raises her eyebrows at me, making me wonder how we're ever going to get rid of the dogs long enough for Free Throw and Catherine to get back to the car. That is, of course, assuming that she's there, and Free Throw can get her out without Hoffman hearing them.

Suddenly, music blares out of the open kitchen window, and I see Tattoo Girl dancing provocatively through the kitchen light. She's thought of everything. Hoffman reaches out and grabs her hair as she disappears from sight. My fingers curl around the door handle but Nikki restrains me. "She knows what she's doing."

"I know," I whisper. "That's the problem."

We wait, unable to see Free Throw in the darkness as he ascends out of the halo of the yardlight. The Dobermans whine and paw, scratch at the wood but they do not bark again. Five minutes turn into eight. The music continues to play, but no figures dance past the window. I try hard not to think of what's going on inside. Eight minutes slip into twelve. "What's taking so long?" I ask Nikki. She has her eyes trained on the staircase. Twelve becomes eighteen. "I'm going in at twenty minutes," I tell her.

"To do what?" she asks. "The dogs will be on you as soon as you get out of the car."

But I can't stand it any longer. Just then sheet lightning flashes on the horizon. Judging by the distant thunder that follows, it's still a long ways away. We wait. Eighteen becomes twenty.

"Look we've got to do something," I say.

"No," she says through gritted teeth. "She'll handle it."

I fight the urge to grab her and shake her, this naive brain beside me. "How the hell would you know?" I snap. "Your life is an academic fairy tale. You're a genius child of high-achieving parents with a hundred percent chance of success ahead of you."

Her eyes stare into the darkness. "I wish," she says softly.

"Right!"

"You don't know what it's like," she whispers between clenched teeth. "Sometimes I think I'll implode from all the pressure."

"From your parents?" I shoot back skeptically.

"From everyone. My paternal grandmother was a Nobel Peace Prize winner. My maternal grandfather has seven buildings and two streets named after him. My parents left Slovakia because they believed I would have more opportunities for excellence here. And so far, all I have done is disappoint." Her body slumps in the seat beside me.

Just then the dogs stand and growl. They leap at the staircase. "Free Throw's coming," I say. "We have to cause a distraction sufficient to attract those killers."

Nikki turns on the dog whistle and I hold Penny's muzzle. One of the dogs bolts towards the car, then races back to the staircase. They burst into a chorus of barks. Free Throw must be on the platform. Work your magic, I think. Work your magic, Free Throw. The house door is flung open and the Dobermans quiet. I feel for the car keys as Hoffman strides out onto the porch. He lifts a shotgun and blasts a shot in the dogs' direction. They scatter and in the glow of the porch light, I notice that his belt buckle dangles from his pant loops. He leans the shotgun beside the door frame when Tattoo Girl stumbles onto the wooden slats beside him. But he stands soldier-like as the sound of an engine reaches our ears.

"What the hell!" screams Hoffman, picking up the gun. "I bet it's those damn cops again." His voice is drowned out as Rigoh's truck cruises into view.

Tattoo Girl shrinks back inside the house, but Rigoh has seen her. I slouch on the front seat beside Nikki. Penny leaps over the seat and whimpers in the back.

As the truck screeches to a stop, Bald Guy cracks the door. The dogs are at his feet immediately.

Hoffman raises the shotgun, but a bullet wedges itself into the wooden siding of the house before he can fire it. Rigoh is balanced on the running board with a handgun. He kicks one of the dogs in the head, then fires another shot. Nikki starts to tremble in the seat beside me.

"You got something that's mine," Rigoh shouts. "Give her back to me and I'll go."

Hoffman raises his arms and the shotgun in the air. "You can have her. Tattooed trash, get out here."

Tattoo Girl does not appear. She fears Rigoh more than Hoffman, that much I know. I glance back at the staircase. Where are Free Throw and Catherine? Then suddenly I see movement. Free Throw leans momentarily into the peripheral glow of the yardlight. I squint past the darkness and realize there is a smaller figure beside him. "Catherine!" I whisper to Nikki.

The dogs encircle Rigoh's truck snarling and barking. Another handgun fires. A canine yelps.

Nikki's eyes are wide discs. This wasn't part of the plan! We look at each other and without a word, I start the car as shouts and gunshots erupt. Nikki shrieks and slides down the seat, visibly shaking.

Don't panic, I tell myself. *Panic only gets you into trouble, not out.* My dad's words. What would he do? I ask myself. How would he navigate this crisis? After all, he did crises. Quickly, I scan our surroundings. Rigoh's truck is between me and the fire escape but nearer the house. For a moment, I contemplate reversing and trying to sneak behind his truck without being noticed. A bullet whizzes over the car's sunroof. My hands shake and Nikki squeals again. *Plan B?* as Dad would say. A bullet hits the tire of Hoffman's beater truck beside us, and I see the vehicle sink. Beside me, Nikki hyperventilates. Past the shed, I tell myself. Around the garden and onto that dirt berm. Maybe it's an old road or at least passable by car. I pull forward until I am beyond the glimmer of the yardlight. A bullet hits our tail light. *Do what you can with what you've got, wherever you are!* I can almost hear Dad talking in my head. "Okay, Dad," I whisper.

Penny's collar jangles. I creep forward. The car bounces as I plow through the long grass beside the shed and bump up onto the raised berm. I turn left away from the barn, in the direction that I drove in from. Holding the steering wheel steady, I let the tires choose their path. The berm seems to be an old overgrown dirt road, and I'm hoping that it leads back to the driveway. It does. Suddenly we can see the corner of the house and the fire escape. It is empty. Damn!

Turning slightly, I angle the car so my headlights illuminate the yard, searching for Free Throw and Catherine. Rigoh is on the running board. Hoffman, with his shotgun raised, is on the porch. A Doberman lies bleeding near the truck tire. There is no sign of Tattoo Girl. Rigoh turns and takes aim at us. I flash my high beams, momentarily blinding him while Nikki tries to find the others. And then I see the back door of the truck open. Billy, Free Throw's brother, stumbles out. A Dobermans lunges at him. Gunshots fly. Billy spins backwards and falls. The dog shrieks. Adrenalin surges through me. I turn right, feeling the crunch of the gravel driveway, and floor the accelerator. Rattling over the Texas gate, I gun the engine, adhering to one of Dad's favourite quotes. *When you're going through hell, speed!*

Nikki curls up on the seat beside me. My hands clench the steering wheel and my leg trembles as I keep the pressure firmly on the gas pedal. We drive to the far edge of the property, and I pull off into the shallow ditch deep under the willow and turn off my lights. The sound of our breathing fills the night air.

"We can't stop here," whispers Nikki. "It's too close."

It's true. Penny puts her paws up on the leather seat and licks my ears. I pull her onto my lap and for a few minutes, we just breathe.

"We can't leave them there," whispers Nikki, and I know she is once again speaking the truth. She presses her face against the glass as I put the car into park.

Images flash in front of me. Guns. Dogs! Billy!

"Did they hit Billy?" My voice is almost a whisper. Even in the darkness, I can see Nikki's ghost-like face. We don't know where Free Throw and Catherine are, and Tattoo Girl is somewhere back there, probably still in the house.

Nikki pulls herself together. "We need to call the police. Now." She reaches for her phone with trembling hands. "Drive, Grady."

She's right, of course, but how long will it take for the police to come? And what will they find when they do? A pale three-quarter moon glows momentarily between fast-moving clouds. I shift into drive, inch forward, then shoulder check, aware in that moment how stupid that must seem. That's when I spot a flash of white. Straining to look backwards, I see it again. "Nikki," I say incredulously. "Is that a horse?"

Nikki drops her phone. She opens the sunroof and peers into the darkness. The wind funnels into the car as the moon reappears.

"Yes, I think it's Margaret!" she cries.

Now we can hear hooves.

The paint mare races parallel to the fence. A truck engine roars to life in the distance. I glance at Nikki but before I can stop her, she's out on the road. "Over here," she screams. The horse changes direction. "Hurry!" Nikki cries as Tattoo Girl approaches the fence.

I turn on the headlights, illuminating the scene momentarily. Nikki stumbles into the ditch and pries the barbed wire strands apart as Tattoo Girl leaps from the horse's bare back. Miraculously, she lands upright, trips towards the fence and ducks between the wires. They scurry up onto the road and reach the car; I extinguish my headlights. And then I hear it; Rigoh's truck is headed this way. I drive the car forward, crashing through the grasses behind the bushes and stop.

# CHAPTER 14

Rigoh's truck barrels past us in the darkness. I try not to notice that Tattoo Girl is partially clothed and instead focus on Nikki's gentle assurances as the two girls sink into the cradle of the back seat.

Nobody moves. When I finally look back, Nikki is holding Tattoo Girl's head against her chest. I slip out of my hoodie and toss it over my headrest. Tattoo Girl pulls it over her head. Her dragon encircles my neck as I plant a kiss on her hand.

"Thanks for waiting," she whispers.

"Of course," I tell her, then ask, "Are you okay?" My voice is filled with angst and immediately I feel her shift.

Her hand clenches and she retracts her arm. There will be no conversation, that is clear. I change the subject. "Where did you learn to ride like that?"

Tattoo Girl adjusts my hoodie sleeves. "That's a long story," she says, breathless.

"And how did you get out?" asks Nikki.

"The front door," Tattoo Girl tells us. "Where are Free Throw and Catherine?"

Quickly, we explain what happened in the yard. "Shit!" is her only response.

That pretty much sums things up. "We need to get the police," Nikki reiterates. She leans over the headrest searching for her phone.

But Tattoo Girl objects. "No! We don't know where Free Throw and Catherine are. Who knows what Hoffman will do if the police show up."

I brace myself for an argument, but Nikki doesn't protest. She is completely out of her depth; we are in Tattoo Girl's territory now.

"Okay, Rigoh's gone, Billy's . . . Billy's either badly hurt at best, dead or gone with Rigoh and Bald Guy. Catherine and Free Throw are somewhere on the property, as is Hoffman," I summarize.

Nikki nods in agreement. It's the best-educated guess we can make.

"How'd you get out?" Tattoo Girl asks me.

"Plan B. We found an old road."

"Nice," Tattoo Girl says.

I wonder if those are my dad's genes, but now's not the time to delve into that. "If you were Free Throw and Catherine, what would you do?" I ask.

"It all depends if he saw Billy go down or not."

Neither Nikki nor I know for sure, but I know Free Throw well enough to know that if he had seen his brother shot, he'd have run right into the gunfire.

"Rigoh got out of that yard pretty fast," says Tattoo Girl.

"Maybe he killed Hoffman," I say.

She shakes her head. "I could hear Hoffman's shotgun firing when Rigoh started the truck."

Nobody wants to hang around when there's been a murder, I figure. Rigoh and Bald Guy split when Billy got hit. So, what would Hoffman do now? Before I can speculate, Tattoo Girl answers my voiceless question.

"He'll either leave now or get rid of the body first. And anyone who might be a witness."

"He can't leave," I say. "At least not until he changes his truck tire. We have to go back."

"Not with the car," says Tattoo Girl. "On foot, now, under the cover of darkness."

"What about the Dobermans?" asks Nikki. "We can't be certain they're incapacitated."

I try to recall the scene in the yard. At least one of them lay dead or dying by the tire. I don't recall any barking after the gunfire. "We'll have to take that chance," I say, stroking Penny's head. "What about Penny? We can't leave her here. What if we don't come back . . . for a while, I mean."

Tattoo Girl reaches for Penny and tucks her inside the pouch of my hoodie. "We'll take her," she says, climbing out of the car. She pulls the blanket off the back seat and wraps it around her torn skirt, securing it at her waist.

Nikki and I join her. The night air is chilly, but the moon is brighter now. Nikki turns up the light on her cell phone and we slip between the rungs of barbed wire and tromp as quickly as possible through the wind-blown grass. "Do you think Catherine and Free Throw are still at the house?" I ask.

"Only if they can't leave," says Tattoo Girl. "Let's go, I'm getting eaten alive."

The mosquitos swarm around her and for a moment, I am reminded of Will. Where is he now? In some European town teaching kids to play computer games and trying to get up enough courage to talk to some Swiss girl? Nikki grips my T-shirt and pulls me along. Lightning forks across the sky, but it is closer now, and the wind is dying. The lull before the storm. We press on.

"Wait," instructs Tattoo Girl. "Can you hear that chink-chink sound?"

I think I hear a vague metallic sound in the distance. "What is it?"

"A shovel. I'm guessing he's burying Billy." She pauses. "Which means Catherine and Free Throw might have gotten away from the house. Let's head to the barn. Maybe we can see more from there."

We can just make out the silhouette of the barn roof when the moonlight tears a rift in the cloud. By the time we reach the trees, the wind is surging, and the rain has started. Thick clouds threaten to usurp the moon. As we approach, I spot the hayloft door under the barn's high peak. Two windows are boarded up on the ground floor. We bend low, sneaking towards the far end of the well-kept structure, out of sight of the house. Suddenly, Penny bounds from Tattoo Girl's pouch and races around the corner of the barn. Catherine staggers towards us; we gather her in a group hug.

"Where's Free Throw?" I ask.

Catherine bursts into tears. "In my grandma's root cellar," she sobs. "I left him there."

"He's dead?" Tattoo Girl asks, her voice catching in her throat.

Catherine shakes her head. "No, unconscious. He's got a wound on his head —" Her voice breaks. I put an arm around her shoulders and wait as she sobs into my shoulder, then gradually regains her composure.

"Now, tell us what happened," I say gently.

Catherine leans against the wooden siding as we duck beneath the barn's overhang out of the rain. "I hit him with a board."

"What?" we ask in unison.

"When his brother fell, he tried to run into the yard." She presses her fingertips together. "I didn't know what else to do." Tears balance on her eyelids.

"It's okay," I whisper.

"I . . . I dragged him down the cellar steps." I notice that her sweater is covered in streaks of blood and dirt. "I couldn't wake him, but I knew I had to get help so I made a run for the shed when the truck took off." She pauses. "Who was that anyway?" She looks from me to Tattoo Girl in the darkness.

"Long story," I say.

"I hid in the shed but I was sure he'd find me." She is on the brink of losing it again but steadies herself against the rough boards as the rain gains momentum. We turn our backs to the storm.

Tattoo Girl gestures towards the barn. "Is there a way in?" she asks.

The huge swing door is on the wall beside us. I sidestep towards it, but it is padlocked with a heavy steel key lock. A hard tug reveals that it is securely bolted shut. "Were there any tools in the shed?" I ask.

"No, Grandpa's workshop was in the barn," says Catherine. She is calmer now, steeling herself to our current dilemma. She joins me outside the door. "Can I borrow your phone?"

I hand it over. She pulls up the light, feels her way along the barn boards, then kneels in front of four heavy canvas flaps near the ground. Without warning, she pushes the flaps aside to reveal a dog door, flattens her tiny frame and squirms through. "I'm in," she calls after a brief silence, "but I'm pretty sure you'd all get stuck." I see the flash of my cell phone through a slit in the barn boards.

"Careful," whispers Nikki. "It may be possible for Hoffman to see the light from the house on the other side. And it would also be advisable to keep our voices down."

Catherine muffles the light. We hear her footsteps shuffle to the opposite end of the barn, then the clink of metal.

Footsteps return, and soon an ancient metal toolbox protrudes from the dog door.

I flip open its latches and search for a crowbar, but Tattoo Girl reaches past me and extracts two large steel wrenches. "Wrenches?" I ask in a confused whisper.

Deftly, she positions one wrench on either side of the lock bridge, about halfway up the arch. The steel sides of the wrench heads touch in the middle. She slides my hoodie sleeves down over her hands then grips the tools tightly and squeezes her wrists together. I watch in amazement as the lock bridge bends outwards then neatly breaks in two at the top. She removes the hook from the latch and passes it to me, along with the wrenches. I tuck them all away in the box and in no time we are inside the dry barn, my wet hands clutching the toolbox. I creak the door shut against the rain as the sweet scent of fresh hay mingles with the earthy smell of oil and dust. Slowly my eyes adjust to the darkness.

"A single cell phone light only," instructs Tattoo Girl in a low whisper.

Catherine shines the beam tentatively across the hay-strewn floor. At the far end is a homemade workbench; an array of large metal tools hang from a peg board and thick dust coats the wooden surface. Stables piled high with rectangular hay bales border both sides of the barn. Only the farthest stable is empty, a metal feeding trough hanging on its outer wall. Catherine shifts the light upwards revealing a wooden railing encasing the hayloft; its wooden floor, supported by large beams, extends halfway over the ground floor the full length of the barn. From below, the only thing visible is more bales of hay stacked against the railing. Catherine leads us to a vertical wooden ladder built into the supporting framework at the building's midpoint. Carefully, we scale it one at a time, Tattoo Girl sliding Penny into the pouch of my hoodie as she climbs. I follow her up, taking the toolbox with me. You never know what we might need to liberate Free Throw. High in the loft, I enter Catherine's sanctuary — a cozy corner niche surrounded by hay.

Two large plastic bins lay in the middle, their lids open. She replaces the lid on one box and shoves it towards the wall. I do the same with the other — a box of electrical parts — recalling that her brother is at a robotics conference. I notice the jars of herbs against the wall. Dusty, torn pillows and blankets are strewn about, and we sink into them. Catherine rests beside me, and I cover her tiny hand with my fingers, marvelling at the courage and strength it took to knock Free Throw out.

Nobody's spoken, but now Tattoo Girl rises and peers through a knothole in the loft door in the direction of the house. "Hoffman will come looking for us," she says. "It's only a matter of time."

Her words hang in the darkness like empty nooses suspended from rafters. How long do we have? Does he know Catherine is no longer upstairs? Are the Dobermans still alive? Will he find Free Throw? A thousand questions clutter my head. I try to think what my father would do. *Focus on one detail at a time, then try and put them together.* "Are the dogs alive?" I ask.

Catherine shakes her head. "He shot them both after the truck left."

"Well, maybe he's not a total asshole," says Tattoo Girl.

I beg to differ. But at least that means the dogs can't track our scent.

Nikki's brain is working overtime. "At this point, Hoffman has likely discovered that Catherine is missing. If he hasn't left yet, there must be a reason."

Catherine shifts uncomfortably. "My grandmother's favourite place on the farm was a flat rock beside the creek," she says.

I'm inclined to cut her off and return to the crisis at hand, but instead, I just listen. I register Nikki and Tattoo Girl's impatience, but we all remain silent. She's been through so much.

"That's where I went first. I needed to pay tribute to my grandmother in my own way."

Not with a traditional funeral, I think, as Catherine continues.

"It was dusk, so I followed the hedge to the barn, but as I got close —" Her voice cracks, "He was here with two rough-looking guys in a black SUV. I don't know what was going on, but he padlocked the barn after the vehicle drove off." She clenches her fingers into a fist. "Then he unchained the dogs." I notice how she never calls Hoffman by name and shiver involuntarily. My arm encircles her shoulders. "They-he-they found me." She doesn't go on, but we all know what happened next.

"I'm calling the police," says Nikki. "Catherine is out of the house."

But Tattoo Girl objects. "What about Free Throw?" Silence descends. "We need to think this through."

Nikki sets her phone in her lap and voices all the thoughts that have already accumulated in her head. "Okay, Hoffman will expect that since the car is gone, Tattoo Girl was not alone, and we have gone to the police." She emphasizes the word *police*, but Tattoo Girl just waves her on. "I imagine he will anticipate that they will arrive shortly, in which case he would want to ensure that there is no evidence of a killing on the property, especially since forensics could easily ascertain if it was his shotgun that killed Billy. After that, I expect he will turn his attention to finding Catherine, who is now missing."

"What if he finds Free Throw?" Desperation creeps into Catherine's voice. "Shouldn't we call for help?"

We should, of course, but she doesn't know that the police are looking for her, that we lied to them about knowing her, or that Reg is in custody for her possible abduction. Now's not the time to fill her in. Besides, we already know that Reg is innocent. Despite our predicament, relief floods over me. But it is short-lived. The wind infiltrates the boards, ambushing the barn. The storm is upon us.

"I think he'll run," says Tattoo Girl as the assault begins.

"He can't drive," I remind her. "His truck has a flat."

"If the police don't come soon, or if he finds the car, he may come looking for us," declares Nikki. Lightning punctuates her sentences. Thunder obliterates her voice and within seconds the deluge of rain begins. We huddle closer together, drawing warmth from the hay and each other.

Rain hurls itself towards the earth. We are playing a waiting game, a potentially deadly one. Lightning electrifies our surroundings. Thunder bellows and the building shakes. The torrent of rain on the metal roof is deafening. A second flash of lightning illuminates four tired and terrified faces. For a moment, everything feels surreal. Light and noise collide above us as the storm dominates the sky. We wait out the onslaught.

"Can Free Throw get out?" asks Tattoo Girl finally, during a lull.

"No, I locked him in from the outside. I thought it was saf—" Thunder expunges her final syllable.

"We need to go back for him. You don't leave a man behind," says Tattoo Girl.

I imagine Free Throw waking up in the root cellar, knowing that Billy is dead and believing we've abandoned him.

What would he do? "He's probably praying for help, right now," I say as the rain surges.

"I doubt that invoking benevolent spiritual guidance at this moment will help him release himself from a locked root cellar," comments Nikki. "And yet, I suspect you are correct, Grady." Forks of light penetrate the slits in the boards. A second thunderstorm cell is moving in.

"We need Hoffman to leave — now. We need to scare him off so we can get to Free Throw." Tattoo Girl has risen and is standing at the knothole watching the storm envelop the land.

Nikki rolls her eyes and I know what she is thinking. What scares a guy like Hoffman?

"Even the walking dead couldn't scare him," says Catherine. "He's the epitome of evil."

"Again," says Nikki, "I'm not sure that a malicious spirit could cause someone to . . . actually, it just might."

We turn curious eyes to her.

"I've been doing a lot of reading on this spiritual, ephemeral stuff," Nikki half-explains. She stands and peers into the box of electrical parts, before beginning to rummage through them.

My stomach grumbles loudly and Catherine gets to her feet. "I wonder," she says and soon she too is rooting around in a plastic box. She extracts six rock-hard granola bars. "It's our emergency supply," she says, grinning. Four bottles of water appear, seals unbroken. It is a feast, and we dig in, smashing the bars inside their wrappers and almost breaking our teeth on them. But at least it is food.

Nikki pulls an old MP3 music player from the box and holds it up triumphantly. But the batteries are dead. Catherine leans into the supply box and pulls out spares. Nikki's eyes sparkle as the storm refuses to relent.

# CHAPTER 15

"Grady, wake up." Nikki jabs me softly in the ribs. Catherine's head leans against my shoulder and I shift, trying not to wake her. Tattoo Girl is asleep on a cushion next to Penny, who whimpers in her sleep. A steady drizzle spits against the roof.

"I require your assistance."

I am groggy, but I rub my eyes as they adjust to the muffled glow of Nikki's cell phone light. Standing, I stretch and peer through the knothole. The storm has passed, and a hazy dawn light is pushing aside the darkness on the horizon like a mysterious hand drawing back a curtain. I think I see a faint light emanating from the house. Nikki holds a metal coat hanger that she has fashioned into a cross. An odd electrical concoction lies in the middle of our circle.

"Okay," she explains. "I've created this cross to use as an antenna. We need to position it close to Hoffman's radio. Then we'll record a message on the MP3 player and use my transmitter to bypass the radio frequencies." She stares at me expecting some reaction, but I am lost. "Oh for goodness' sake, Grady, with this we can override any radio station and transmit a message from the walking dead through Hoffman's radio."

I take a minute to process what she is saying. "So, it will be like he's hearing a ghost on his radio?"

"Exactly."

"That's brilliant!" I exclaim. "How did you think of that?"

Nikki sighs. "As usual, the original idea cannot be attributed to me. I read about this program in Europe where they used a similar device to deter reckless and drunk driving at high-risk accident locations that had already claimed innocent lives."

I take a seat. "So drivers would hear the ghostly voices of the dead and slow down."

"That was the hope, but I didn't investigate further to see how effective it was. I would hypothesize that . . ." Her voice trails off. "Anyway, that's not important now, Grady. Time is of the essence." She drops the contraption in front of me. "First, we need to record a message on the MP3 player from Billy. And since that is impossible and Hoffman has no idea what Billy sounds like, we need your voice."

Everyone is awake by this time. Nikki fills them in on her plan.

"What do I say?" I ask.

"Something that will make Hoffman fear he will be found out," says Tattoo Girl.

"How about this," I suggest. "Your bullet pierced my body, but my spirit is not dead. You buried my flesh . . ." I pause.

"In the garden," says Catherine softly.

We turn to her.

"I-I watched him from the shed." She chokes the words out as Nikki looks up, horrified. The pencil lead she is using to scribe on a scrap of paper breaks. I wonder how long Catherine's nightmares will last.

Nikki digs up another pencil and writes *in the garden* as Tattoo Girl adds "But my soul will not die!"

I stare at her.

"What?" she says. "He was Catholic."

Nikki sets the paper in front of me. I read it with vehemence and add, "You will pay for your evil ways."

Once it has been recorded, Nikki gathers her creation. I stuff my phone into my jeans pocket and seek clarification about the second phase of this operation. "The root cellar is at the base of the fire escape, correct?"

"Yes, the original homestead's kitchen was there," says Catherine. "I hope Free Throw's alright."

Nikki and I descend the ladder and slip through the door, pulling it shut behind us. "We need to be within one hundred metres of the house," says Nikki as we slink forwards.

I hesitate; that's definitely within gunshot range.

"Come on," she urges. "We just have to place this contraption, not stay there with it. What do you think I am, utterly reckless and completely foolhardy?"

Raindrops leach from the grasses in the ditches as we avoid the puddles and mud on the dirt road. The air is crisp after the storm and I shiver, but my trembling increases as the house comes into view.

"What if he doesn't have the radio on?" A wave of panic washes over me. How could Nikki neglect such an important detail!

"I have a backup plan," she whispers, "but it is probable that he will be listening for updates on weather or news if he hasn't already left the premises."

We retrace Catherine's steps in reverse, obscuring ourselves in the hedge, passing the overgrown garden that now conceals Billy's body. Our pants and shoes are soaked when we finally cross the road and duck behind the shed. From there, we can see the back porch and door of the house but still stay out of view. The faint crackle of the radio reaches our ears, and I give Nikki a thumbs up. She points at an old wheelbarrow halfway to Hoffman's truck, then gives me a thumbs up and creeps towards it using Hoffman's old beater as a blind. I stand guard outside the shed as she jams the antenna attached to the MP3 transmitter into the wheelbarrow, makes some quick adjustments and retreats. I flash her a proud smile as she rejoins me. If I strain, I can hear Billy's ghost. We crouch behind the shed and wait as the sun sets its sights on the eastern horizon.

Minutes later, the kitchen door slams open and an ATV engine rumbles to life at the side of the house. Peering around the corner of the shed, we watch Hoffman speed down the driveway, without looking back. I hug Nikki as the roar recedes. But it's not over yet.

When silence once again prevails, Nikki and I cautiously venture towards the house. The door is ajar. The bodies of the dogs lie in a bloody heap. My voice fills the kitchen as we draw close, the ghostly threat emanating from the radio again and again.

Nikki retrieves her contraption and the threats cease. We race towards the root cellar. "Free Throw," I call down as I dislodge the sliding bolt that serves as a lock. We pull the two trap doors open.

Free Throw's eyes, like full moons, look up at us. I notice that his shirt is stained with blood and immediately spot the gash on his head. His clothes are drenched and his body trembles.

"Thank God," he calls as I step gingerly down the rotting stairs to help him out. "I-I-Billy's dead," he wails suddenly, collapsing against me.

"Free Throw," I say trying to emulate my father's crisis voice. "Right now, I just need you to put one foot in front of the other and climb these stairs with me." I place one of his arms over my shoulder and hold his wrist as he stumbles upward, his feet slipping on the wet, rotting boards and his body swaying. Finally, we reach the top of the staircase and Nikki's outstretched hands. We catch our breath outside the cellar. "We're not gonna talk yet, we're just gonna walk. Okay?" I say. He nods. The three of us stagger forward in the direction of the barn, focusing on the rhythm of our feet rather than the thoughts in our heads.

I swing the barn door open and Penny scampers towards us. The girls meet us at the door and help Free Throw up the ladder, with Nikki close behind. Just as I reach the top, Tattoo Girl places a finger against her lips. Within seconds, I hear it too. The whir of a car engine. "The cops?" I whisper, stumbling over the last rung. But she shakes her head and gestures with gloved hands towards Catherine.

Catherine is kneeling on the blankets surrounded by the others, a canvas duffel bag in their midst. On the hay in front of them sits a rectangular metal box lined with felt. Nine handguns and four boxes of ammunition lay on the blankets.

"What the . . . ?" I ask.

Tires crunch over wet gravel and Nikki darts to the knothole. "They're at the house," she whispers. She glares at Tattoo Girl. "Where did these firearms come from?"

"I figured there had to be something illegal going on if the barn was locked and he held Catherine," Tattoo Girl mutters. "So we went looking. There are two more duffel bags in the feed trough."

Car doors slam and an engine purrs to life. Fear grips me in an intractable hold.

"We need to get out of here now!" Nikki's voice is adamant.

But Tattoo Girl shakes her head. "It's too late. There's only one way out and that's the way they'll come in."

Free Throw crouches behind the hay bales as I reach for a box of bullets. "Then we have to put them back."

But Tattoo Girl slaps my hand away. "That's evidence," she growls, "and we're not exactly the most credible witnesses." Her gloved hand hurriedly picks up a firearm, and I wonder how she had the wherewithal to think about all these details.

Car tires bump towards us. There isn't time. "Just give me the empty box," I insist.

"No, they will detect the weight discrepancy," says Nikki. She grabs Catherine's grandfather's toolbox, shoves it into the duffel and almost throws it at me. "Go!"

I practically leap from the loft and bolt to the trough. Car doors click shut outside the barn. As I slide the duffel into the feed trough beside the other two, the door hinges squeak. I dive towards the hay bales in the adjacent stable and scramble up them, flattening my body on the top behind two raised bales. I can't see the intruders, so I'm praying they can't see me. But if they reach the trough, I'll be visible.

"He said he'd be here," says a deep voice. Footsteps enter the barn and a slice of dawn accompanies them.

"He's a chickenshit," returns an Irish accent.

Just then Penny darts out of the workshop growling. The girls must have brought her down with them when they found the guns. A gun fires and a half-scream escapes from me before I clamp my lips shut. The dog's paws scurry away.

"Put the gun away," says the deep voice. "We don't want the neighbours showing up."

"I thought I heard a scream."

Adrenalin floods every cell of my body. "It was probably that stupid dog," comes the reply.

I squirm in the direction of the door, pausing every few inches trying to minimize the rustling. I glance upwards. Free Throw's terrified eyes peer at me between hay bales but none of the girls is visible. I inch my way sideways. The safest place in the barn right now is outside.

"They're all here." The deep voice hails from the trough area.

I slide to the edge of the hay under the cover of footsteps as the Irish man moves in that direction. The door is within reach, but I don't dare thud off the bales onto the wooden floor without another distraction. Then I hear it. A faint robin's whistle from the loft. Free Throw!

"What was that?" asks the Irish man.

"A bird," says the deep voice. "It's dawn."

The whistle comes again, and Penny darts into the light of the door, her bark filling the barn. I let my sneakers thud softly onto the floor, pressing my back against a recessed hay bale as the men's footsteps pursue the dog. Penny sprints out the open door and the men return to the trough.

"We should open the bags," suggests the Irish guy.

"We should vamoose before it gets to be daylight," says the other.

I can't stay where I am because I'll be visible from the exit. As they gather the bags, I slip outside, positioning myself behind the swing door, just metres from the back of their SUV. I check out the terrain, but it's too exposed to make a run for it and their footsteps are already close. Commanding my heart to beat more quietly, I stay put, hoping they aren't the type to close up when they leave. But if I can see them, then I might be able to identify them or their vehicle. Quickly, I pull my phone out of my pocket and snap a photo of the SUV's licence plate. The men reach the car, pop the trunk and place the duffel bags inside. Doors close and tires slosh down the muddy road.

I wait until birdsong announces the morning, then dart inside and scurry back up the ladder. Free Throw offers me a hand at the top, pulling me into his shoulder. I mutter a soft "Thanks, man."

Quickly I explain what happened and show them the photo. Nikki types frantically. "I'm notifying the police," she says, then glances at Tattoo Girl, "on the anonymous tip line."

Tattoo Girl nods. She has finished repacking the guns and ammunition. "Let's go!" she says, picking up the latched box. Apparently, we are taking the evidence with us.

We scramble down the ladder where Penny awaits us and I am glad to see that the little dog appears unharmed and in good spirits. I scoop her up and lead the way. We are on high alert as we exit the barn, but Free Throw's eyes glaze over as we pass the house and dead dogs. "My brother," he moans. We pull him along through the field to the Audi with its broken tail light. It is where I left it — with tires intact — and I sigh with relief as I reach for the keys in my pocket. Free Throw tucks Penny into the back seat, and Tattoo Girl and I wedge the box of guns in the trunk.

As the first shafts of sunshine penetrate the clouds on the horizon, we climb into the car, reverse out of the bushes and drive back to the city. Nikki turns the radio to classical music. It is a subtle request for silence, and we honour it. I glance sideways at her and then into the rearview mirror. Catherine and the members of the Nothing Club. Four juvenile delinquents in community service.

I almost snort aloud. Like it's done any good at all in reforming us. Free Throw just committed his second break and enter, Nikki's done more hacking in the last two days than she's probably ever done, Tattoo Girl's compromised herself, and as for me, well, simple arson looks good after this.

"How did Rigoh find us?" Tattoo Girl asks Nikki quietly once we are safely on the highway. "You turned off that feature on my phone and he still found us."

Nikki ponders a moment. "Did he have access to your Google account?"

"I-I'm guessing so. Why?"

"He likely used Google Map timeline to figure out where you'd been in the last twenty-four hours, then retraced all your steps until he located the farm."

Tattoo Girl tosses her device on the front seat. "I need a new phone."

"Not until we turn the current one over to the police," says Nikki.

But as I reach the city limits, Tattoo Girl pipes up. "To Mrs. Stafford's," she says. "We have to drop Penny." Then she adds, "It might be good to clean up a bit first."

Nikki doesn't argue. "It might also be wise to relate consistent stories to the police," she states.

When we arrive at Mrs. Stafford's, I park the car in the garage, leave the evidence securely locked in the trunk and refrain from looking at the damage to the back end. We huddle together in the family room then disperse. Catherine cleans Free Throw's wounds and Tattoo Girl takes a shower. I pluck hay from my hair in front of the hall mirror. Free Throw sits outside with Walter and Penny. Nikki, as usual, is on her phone when I return to the family room.

"What are you doing now?" I ask. The adrenalin is seeping out of me like a balloon rapidly deflating. I am exhausted.

"Do you think Mrs. Stafford knows who Reg really is?" she asks.

I am on full alert again. "She-she must," I stammer.

Nikki shrugs.

"If she doesn't, then this is all just too bizarre and . . ." I search for the right word. "Ominous."

## CHAPTER 16

"Ready?" says Tattoo Girl, rejoining us and running her fingers through her damp hair. She is wearing a floral print dress that must belong to Mrs. Stafford and she looks so . . . innocent. I wonder what she hasn't told us and if she ever will.

"Yes. The police are looking for us," says Nikki as we all gather in the family room. "The fact that we are all unaccountably absent from our homes is highly suspicious. We'll each have to give statements so it might be prudent if we are all on the same page."

"Let's start with what happened Friday," Tattoo Girl says throwing a long look at Catherine.

Catherine's embarrassment is obvious, but she obliges. "I told Reg I was going to Scott's — the asshole."

Tattoo Girl snickers and I feel my heart leap in my chest.

"I didn't want anyone to be able to find me, at least not right away, so after Reg drove off, I took the bus to Ridgeview and hiked out to the farm."

My voice is low and even. "You forgot to cancel your hair appointment."

Catherine startles. "How do you know that?"

"And they found your glasses at Reg's apartment," says Nikki.

Catherine's eyebrows arch. "So that's where I lost them. I put them in the top compartment of my backpack so I could take my contacts out, but when I got to the bus station they were gone."

I recall her playing with the zipper while she sat on the curb.

"They must have fallen out in Reg's car. His back seat was full of boxes with stuff to repair," she adds.

"So when he pulled the boxes out, Catherine's glasses fell to the pavement," I deduce. Even the improbable can be true sometimes, I think, catching Nikki's eye.

"Will somebody tell me what's going on here," demands Catherine.

Tattoo Girl gives her a scaled-down version of what's happened since Reg dropped her at Scott's place. The colour drains from her face when she learns that Reg was detained, but she half-smiles as Tattoo Girl tells her about our sleuthing and then our decision to go find her.

"I had no idea they'd arrest Reg," Catherine admits. "My intent was to stay in the hayloft for the night and return after the funeral." She tucks her feet under her. "But the dogs found me, and the next thing I knew I was gagged and tied to the bed frame upstairs." She breathes heavily, momentarily lost in that distressing memory. "After the cops showed up, he came upstairs ultra-agitated." Her fingers rub the back of her neck, and I'm amazed she's holding it all together. "Kept interrogating me about where I'd been on the property and who was with me. There were some pretty heated phone discussions downstairs afterwards, but I couldn't hear any details."

"Did he hurt you?" I ask, almost inaudibly.

She shakes her head, and we all exhale relief. "I heard your voices when you drove in, but I couldn't call out and then you left." She blinks back tears. "But then you returned, and suddenly Free Throw was at the window." She smiles gratefully at him. "After that, gunshots erupted and . . . all I remember is half-falling down that rickety old fire escape and jumping off the platform."

Free Throw holds up his bandaged hand. "Getting out wasn't so hard. Getting in was the tough part."

"You smashed the window with your bare hand?" I say.

Free Throw nods. "Probably not something I'd do again."

Tattoo Girl's eyes have a knowing look, but I don't know what she knows. She twists her mouth in annoyance. "So, what happened outside the house, Grady?" she asks.

I want to ask her what happened inside the house, but I don't. Instead, I give her a recap. "We couldn't get out the way we drove in, so we followed that dirt road that runs in front of the barn around to the driveway. We saw Catherine and Free Throw on the staircase and blinded Rigoh with our high beams hoping they could reach us."

Tattoo Girl gives me a private smile. "Pretty clever for a wuss," she says.

Nikki jumps in. "We were adhering to the plan, but then Billy stepped out of the vehicle and chaos ensued." She glances at Free Throw. "It didn't appear that he was armed."

Free Throw rubs his temples. "Billy hated guns," he says. "My brother was as peaceful as they come." He glances up and asks, "Do you think my mom knows?"

I shrug.

"I gotta tell her," he announces, rising to his feet. But Tattoo Girl restrains his arm. It is an oddly tender touch for a dragon and Free Throw stops in his tracks. His eyes close. For a moment, I think he will start to sing like he did last time. Instead, he paces. The easy grace with which he moves is gone. He is unnerved and fragile like a butterfly on the ground which, when stepped on, will turn to dust. Penny watches and whimpers.

Tattoo Girl returns to Tattoo Girl. "When I saw Rigoh's truck, I bolted out the front door, straight for the paint mare in the paddock. I could hear the shots in the yard so I just rode, hard. And then I heard Nikki yelling and found you two in the car by the willow."

"When did you learn to ride like that?" Nikki asks, reiterating my earlier question.

Tattoo Girl's voice becomes nostalgic. "I rode a lot when I was younger. Me and my twin sister." I notice a small rip in her veil.

"Beth," says Nikki softly.

Tattoo Girl nods. She traces the pattern on Mrs. Stafford's throw pillow. "My mother was from Cambodia. My dad met her there when he worked for Christian Global Doctors." At least that explains her Christian background. "My mom found him and Jesus and followed them both to Canada."

This is a lot of information from Margaret. There is a long still silence before she speaks again.

"Beth and I were inseparable. Then one day, lightning spooked my horse and there was an accident . . ." Her voice trails off. We wait. She looks up and gives us a classic Tattoo Girl dismissal. "And then I lost Beth."

It hits me like lightning. Suddenly, I understand the guilt she wears, the remorse and responsibility that drag her into the streets, into the lion's den. "It wasn't your fault," I tell her. "You don't control where lightning strikes."

Tattoo Girl scowls at me. "Of course, it wasn't my fault. And it wasn't Beth's either. My horse was spooked, out of control."

I pull back. "Yes, but Beth didn't die because . . ."

"What," she says with scornful impatience, "are you talking about? Beth didn't die."

"She didn't?"

"Beth didn't die," she repeats. "I did." Tattoo Girl's words explode into the room, then threaten to blow the roof off the house. "They pronounced me dead at the hospital," she tells us, then shrugs. "Except here I am."

Nikki blinks rapidly. "In which case, you were clinically dead before miraculously returning to life."

Tattoo Girl nods. "For almost three minutes."

"H-How?" I stammer.

"I don't know, Grady. I was looking down at my body on that table in the emergency room. I could see them working on me, then pronounce me dead. And all I wanted to do was go towards this beautiful light above me."

"The light of God," says Free Throw.

"And then, just like that, I was being pulled back into my body. It wasn't my time, I guess. Apparently, it happens."

"Apparently," I repeat. I try not to think of my father, but it is all I can think of. Was it his time? Could he have come back?

"Wow," says Catherine finally. "That must have been . . . so strange."

Tattoo Girl sighs. "They kept me overnight at the hospital. Then I went home. Life returned to normal, except then both my father and Christianity lost their appeal for my mother. A day after our thirteenth birthday, she went back to Cambodia and never returned. I haven't heard from her since." She opens her palm, revealing the rose bush adorned with birds.

I steal a glance at her. What mother abandons her daughter? Daughters?

She stares into space. "She took Beth with her." The veil tears a little farther.

"You didn't want to go?" asks Catherine.

Tattoo Girl digs her long nails into the throw pillow. "I wasn't invited."

The veil is completely torn away now. Free Throw's mouth gapes. I clutch my stomach as if I've just been sucker-punched, and Tattoo Girl's lovebirds disappear into a thorny fist. "I left shortly afterwards," she adds, bringing us up to date.

And lived on the streets until she moved in with Rigoh. "Then why the guilt?" I ask, referring to her admission on the swing. "Shouldn't that belong to your mother?"

Tattoo Girl's pewter eyes pin me to my chair. "You think she just flipped a coin to decide which one of us to take?"

We fall silent. "That's shitty," says Free Throw at last.

Tattoo Girl bites her pierced lip then flashes us a forced smile. "Well," she says donning her street armour voice again, "sometimes shit happens."

"Yeah," acknowledges Free Throw as I try to evade the emotions that threaten to smother me. How could you ever rationalize being left when your twin was chosen?

Free Throw's voice slices through my thoughts. "My life's been shit from the moment the kitten died —"

"That is shit," says Tattoo Girl. "And it's time you let that story go."

His tall form shrivels.

"What gives?" I ask feeling a prickle of anger. The guy's just lost his brother, after all.

But Tattoo Girl isn't backing down. "You didn't break into that warehouse to rescue a kitten. You didn't break into that warehouse at all." Silence stretches tightly across the room. "Any idiot knows you don't smash a window with your bare hand. It's the first rule of B and E. And if you'd done it in the warehouse, you wouldn't have done it again last night." She pauses. "Billy knew it when he broke into that warehouse looking for a drug drop, didn't he?"

For a moment, I fear Free Throw will slam out the door, away from her accusations. But when he makes a motion, it is only with his lips. "It was his second offence. If he'd taken the rap for it, he'd have gone to jail. I had no choice."

"We always have a choice," says Tattoo Girl. "You chose to take the heat for him." She pauses then adds quietly, "If Billy had gone to jail, he might still be here."

Free Throw's shoulders twitch. "I had to," he says. "I'm the reason he's dead." A sob dams his throat, then his words flood the room. "I brought the drugs home first." Tears stream down his face and suddenly I know why he wonders if God forgives all. And now, he has Billy's death on his conscience too.

But Tattoo Girl is unmoved. "But you didn't get hooked, Free Throw. You got out. You made a choice."

"I knew the Lord wouldn't approve," says Free Throw softly, and I am struck once again by how his faith has benefited him even as it holds him hostage. "So did Billy, but he didn't have the strength."

Tattoo Girl relents. "Addiction isn't a choice," she acknowledges, a statement that Nikki looks like she will confirm with an outpouring of statistics. This time, she refrains. Tattoo Girl looks up at each of us in turn. "We all made stupid choices."

She is, I know, correct.

Nikki's phone beeps and she sticks her earbuds in. "We should probably check in at the police station," she suggests. I am struck by how chill she sounds. "Reg might appreciate it."

Once again, I am behind the wheel of Mrs. Stafford's no longer pristine Audi. As I stop in the No Parking zone in front of the station, I add it to the list of laws I've already broken while in community service.

Catherine is the first to disembark. "I'm going in first," she says bravely. "Alone. I'm the one they're looking for."

And she can fully exonerate Reg! I drive slowly around the block, then park illegally again, and we go in, leaving the guns in the trunk. The police can handle those.

Immediately, we are met by a ring of police officers and parents. My mother throws her arms around me and cries. Nikki's father is there too. He is an aloof grey-haired man with an edge to him. Her mother could be Nikki's older twin. She has the same blond hair and angular features. They do not embrace their daughter as Nikki apologizes profusely for disappointing them once again. If they only knew what she has done in the past thirty-six hours!

Tattoo Girl's father arrives in his tailored suit and shiny leather shoes. He stares at her as if he does not know who she is. He does *not* know who she is. Free Throw's mother shows up with two of his siblings. They crawl into their big brother's lap, and from his expression, I know they have heard the news of Billy. I cross the floor and offer him my hand. He takes it and pulls me into his shoulder. It feels like a rock, and I wonder where the dusty butterfly has gone in such a short time. Catherine emerges from an examining room and her mother and father approach her tentatively.

It takes almost five hours to have us all give separate statements, but nobody leaves when we are finished. The officers have retrieved the guns and ammunition from the Audi's trunk and are busy documenting the evidence in another room. Mom has sub sandwiches delivered to the station, politely refusing Tattoo Girl's dad's offer of a hundred-dollar bill. We sit in the waiting room until the police release Reg. And when he walks through the doors, we mob him like he is some kind of Olympian. He takes each of our hands and I am certain that Mrs. Stafford knows his real identity. She must! But neither Nikki nor I ask. That is a question for Mrs. Stafford. We do our best to fill Reg in on what has happened without reliving it all until a uniformed officer finally whistles us into silence.

"We have trauma counsellors available," he tells us. "And we would urge you all to utilize this free resource. Please see Constable Walters to set up appointments." He points towards a desk at the rear of the room.

While our parents make these arrangements, we huddle together with Reg. "When can we come back to work?" I ask.

A look of concern spreads over his face. "How about you take this week to rest up," he declares, "and return to Glenmeadows next Monday? If you want to." His hand closes over Free Throw's. "But there's no obligation, you hear."

Free Throw nods. His loss is so much greater than ours.

Reg clears his throat. "I'd like to paint the shed. Make it into the Nothing Club headquarters, so you four had better start thinking of design ideas."

I feel Catherine tense up beside me. She reaches into her shorts pocket and turns to the police officer standing nearby. "Officer," she says. "I stole fifty dollars from the concession at the pool last Friday. I wish to be charged." She extends the fifty-dollar bill in her hand towards the cop. I know it's a lie, but I can't help smiling. Her parents look aghast; the officer stutters but has no idea what to do.

And then Free Throw laughs. His laughter dances through the sunlight and over the sombre faces of our parents. He throws an arm around Catherine's shoulders and drags her into our midst. We all laugh and embrace her. "Welcome to the Nothing Club," I say.

## CHAPTER 17

We file out of the station, but not before I arrange to meet Nikki after supper. Mom wants me to rest that evening, but when I insist on seeing Mrs. Stafford, she even offers me a lift and goes out of her way to pick up Nikki. As we drive, I try to ignore the ominous feeling in my gut. Mrs. Stafford must know who Reg really is! But if she doesn't, well that's just too freaky to contemplate. She's still on Unit 81, so we march upstairs. I grasp Nikki's hand and she squeezes mine in return. "Reg's arrest made the news," I remind her.

"Yes," says Nikki. Mrs. Stafford is awake and delighted to see us. Immediately I notice that she has no television. She asks how Reg's flu is and Nikki tells her, "About the same."

We politely inquire about her elbow, and she informs us that the surgery was successful, but she has an infection, hence the IV bag that drips into her veins. "The antibiotics knock me out and make me a little loopy," she says with a laugh. "You caught me at a good time."

Nikki nods. Her pale fingers intertwine.

I don't want to know, but I have to. My voice cuts to the core, like Nikki's apple invention. "Mrs. Stafford, I don't mean to shock you, but the man who killed your daughter. He's here. He's Reg."

Mrs. Stafford looks puzzled for a minute. Then she reaches for her ice water and sips through the straw as if she hasn't heard my words. "Oh yes, Grady," she says finally. "I know."

"So, he didn't kill Adrianna?"

"Oh yes, he did." She pushes away the Styrofoam glass. "I know this must seem strange to you, but since you obviously know part of the story, you may as well know the rest."

She motions towards two chairs beside the bed, and we take a seat. "Reg kidnapped my Adrianna after his wife and daughter were killed in a car crash. He was distraught and my daughter looked very much like his little girl, Patricia. He had gone on stress leave from his job and had started seeing a grief counsellor at an office not far from Adrianna's school. One day, he drove past the school and saw her. He hit the brakes and bolted out of the car, almost getting hit himself. He was so sure it was his own little girl. That afternoon and every day for the next two weeks, he followed her bus to and from school. He told me that it was all he had left to hang onto."

She sips her water and continues. "Then one day, the wind blew Adrianna's hat away while she was waiting for the bus. He got out to retrieve it, and according to Reg, something just snapped in his brain. He told her the bus wasn't coming and he could drive her to school. It was a kidnapping, only he wasn't going to hold her for ransom. He just wanted her with him. He wanted Patricia with him one more time."

"We had no word for hours and then the police got a tip. They went to Reg's street and knocked on doors, but he had Adrianna in his wife's painting studio at the back of the property. The police didn't check it, but Reg worried they might be watching, so he didn't take her food until very late. It was her favourite — grilled cheese with lots of mayo." She laughs softly and yawns. Her eyes are heavy.

"What happened?" I prompt.

"She was restrained so she wouldn't run away. He didn't understand Adrianna's diabetes, so he didn't think it would be too much trouble to wait until night to deliver her supper. Her sugars got low, and she slipped into a coma. He found her that night and tried to revive her, but it was too late. He was the one who called the ambulance."

I can't keep the lump out of my throat. Nikki blinks furiously and I realize she is on the verge of tears. Where has the emotionless scientist gone?

"It was very hard," Mrs. Stafford tells us. "Reg pleaded guilty to manslaughter, so there was no trial, but my husband was livid. He wanted the death penalty, but Reg got life. Six months later, we received a letter of apology. My husband tore it to shreds."

Mrs. Stafford yawns again. She will fade soon. I lean forward. "Eventually, I learned to accept our loss, but my husband never forgave. We moved to Canada, but it didn't help. I think it is perhaps why he got cancer — the stress was too much. When he died, Reg saw the obituary and sent a sympathy card. That was when I decided to write back. For ten years Reg and I corresponded. Once he had served his time, I arranged for him to come to Canada. The house and yard were too much for me to maintain, and I wanted him to have a new start."

I am shocked. How could anyone forgive the way she has?

"What was that like?" asks Nikki. "Seeing him again?"

Memory steals over Mrs. Stafford. "It was difficult," she says. "But it was the right thing to do. He's been a wonderful friend."

That part we know is true. The rest boggles my mind.

"You see," she says, "we've made our peace. We made it long ago." She shifts, trying to stay awake. I wonder if I could ever forgive like she has. "It was because of my experience with Reg that I got involved with the community service supervision program. It changed my view about a lot of things."

"So technically you supervise us?" I say, recalling Tattoo Girl's words.

"Technically yes," she says, "but over the years, it's fallen more and more to Reg. He's so good with kids, so accepting and non-judgemental."

We nod. There is really nothing else to say unless we want to tell Mrs. Stafford about Reg having been in custody. I look around the room. Maybe she already knows. "Have you been following the news?" I ask casually.

She shakes her head." This is the longest I've been awake, I think. Why?"

I shrug as her eyelids grow heavy, then rise and squeeze her hand. "I guess we should go." She is for all intents and purposes, asleep.

That night, I open my bottom dresser drawer and pull a framed picture of my father out. I stare at it for a long moment, then replace it in the drawer and crawl into bed.

And so, we are five the next week at work. None of us talks about the week off, our counselling sessions, our losses or what's happened. We are craving normalcy. Our only job is to paint the shed with whatever design we care to come up with. Catherine doesn't work the concession. Instead, Reg arranges for Scott to do so while his boss lifeguards. We make a point of ordering frozen treats and changing our minds a dozen times.

By mid-morning, we have painted *The Nothing Club* on the shed wall, but nothing else. We all have notepads, but we can't figure out what to draw. Nothing is the concept of the absence of anything. Nil plus nil equals nil. Nought times nought equals nought. Nothing divided by nothing is impossible. "In fact," Nikki tells us, "since nothing is the absence of something, it is impossible to assign a value to it."

"Which makes it priceless," I say.

"Perhaps we should consider sketching elements of our individual journeys that resulted in our becoming members of this elite club," suggests Nikki, picking up a notepad. It's as good a suggestion as any, so we scribble designs and ideas on notepads for a while. Symbols representing our individual journeys. Free Throw draws a bandaged hand cradling a kitten, and Catherine settles on a fifty-dollar bill and a jar of herbs. Tattoo Girl's horse rearing in front of Rigoh's truck is impressive, and she helps Nikki draw a lifelike brain to encase her cell phone. I sketch a firefighter's hat beneath a Christmas tree but flip my sketch face down as the others reveal their drawings.

Tattoo Girl stares hard at me. "Well?" she asks finally. "You going to bare your soul like the rest of us or do I have to beat it out of you?"

Relief floods over me. I thought I'd never have to tell. "My dad was a firefighter, and he worked Christmas Eve. I was pissed off because we had to wait until the morning to open gifts." I take a deep breath and exhale my words. "So I told him that I hoped he died in a fire that night . . . and he did."

"I'm sorry, Grady," says Catherine and her hand brushes my shoulder. "But it's not your fault."

I smile at her gratefully. It's true that I didn't cause that fire; I didn't make the floorboards collapse, but I still wonder.

His captain implied at the eulogy that Dad heroically knew he might die, and he went in anyway. Did he choose, I wonder? Between those people and me — after I'd been such a jerk. Did he see that bright light and have a choice like Tattoo Girl?

I toss my sketch onto the grass with the rest of the drawings. All we have to do is paint them onto the shed now, but something doesn't feel right.

"A central image that unifies them and embodies all that we have learned would greatly enhance this project," observes Nikki. It's a tall order but she's right.

"Fireworks!" The thought blasts into my head.

Tattoo Girl's eyes light up. She pulls up an image of six colourful detonations of light in the night sky on her phone. "With one of our symbols in the centre of each light burst."

"Because we blew up our lives with bad choices," says Free Throw.

"Because we're finally ridding ourselves of the negativity we've carried for so long," counters Catherine.

"With our new optimism appropriately represented by eruptions of light," adds Nikki.

"That are remarkably beautiful." Tattoo Girl's eyes sparkle with artistic inspiration.

"Especially when you see them all together," I conclude.

Tattoo Girl paints explosions of colour on the shed as we lounge in the shade. A kaleidoscope of light bursts fills the wall like giant dandelion puffs falling upwards. Then each of us adds our symbol to the centre of a firework. I choose a vivid yellow flare like my father's helmet. Finally, Tattoo Girl adds portraits of Walter and Penny in the background, streams of light encircling their necks like leashes. We stand back and admire our work. It is truly a thing of beauty. Walter sniffs, then pees on it.

"What about Reg?" Free Throw and I ask simultaneously.

"What about me?" asks Reg arriving with Penny. He emits a low, appreciative whistle as he takes in our design, and Penny goes crazy. We all burst into laughter. With our encouragement, he adds a drawing of his own to a shimmering white burst — an insulin syringe and a hearse.

"So much guilt and shame," says Catherine standing back to look at our artwork.

Reg shifts his stance. "Actually, I see fear."

"Fear?" I ask. I'm with Catherine on the guilt and shame page.

"Fear of not being forgiven, fear of not being enough or who we're supposed to be, fear of acknowledging our true selves. Often, we're not even aware of those fears because they are embedded in our subconscious." He bends to pet Walter. "I've been there — on all counts," he explains. "In the end, it all comes down to feeling unworthy." I glance around at the four faces beside me and can tell that Reg's words have resonated with more than just me.

"When our sense of self isn't strong, we tend to make bad choices, like the ones that landed you all here." Reg pets Walter, who groans happily. "Fortunately, eventually, we have to face the fact that things aren't working. To bring about real change, we often need to understand our subconscious fears." Walter rolls onto his back and his hind leg revs into action as Reg finds his scratch spot.

"But if they are subconscious," says Nikki slowly, "we aren't aware of them until we bring them to consciousness." Her gaze meets Reg's. "Expanded consciousness!"

"Through our failures, we become vulnerable, which leads us to deeper connections with ourselves and others. That boosts our sense of self-worth and gives us a new way forward, with support along the way."

It's a lot of words for Reg, so I know they must be important.

"You got that right," says Free Throw. "We're thick as thieves."

"Or maybe carjackers," I add glibly.

"Speaking of that," Reg tells us, "the cops arrested Rigoh and his bald sidekick. They are both in custody and I don't think they'll be out anytime soon. And they picked up Hoffman thanks to your anonymous tip and Grady's photo. Apparently, he gave up the smugglers and the cops unearthed an additional cache of illegal weapons."

We high-five, then sit in the shade. Tattoo Girl touches up some of the painting as I contemplate Reg's words. I'm not the same person I was when I showed up here. None of us is. Have I found a new way forward? Have I forgiven myself? Has Dad forgiven me, wherever he or his spirit is? "So how does spirituality fit into all this?" I blurt out.

"It's different for everyone," Reg says. "But the way I look at it, when we believe in something greater than us, whether it's God, or the universe or whatever, then we see ourselves as part of something good that — even if we can't understand it with our senses — connects us all. Something that helps us see our similarities instead of our differences. I think spirituality helps us respond to ourselves and each other without judgement, in a more compassionate manner."

"So we're able to forgive more easily," says Free Throw, "and be forgiven." He looks visibly relieved.

I scrutinize the shed, while Tattoo Girl studies Nikki. "So, what do you say, Nikki Wiki, are you a believer in spirituality now?"

We all want to know, but uncharacteristically, Nikki takes her time answering. "Scientifically speaking, logic and spirituality don't belong in the same sentence," she begins. "And yet, there are certain things I know now that make me question science in this regard."

We all hold our breath.

"First, it is difficult to explain the unlikely connection I feel with the four of you, given our diverse backgrounds and beliefs." Tattoo Girl snorts and I chuckle. "Second, for some inexplicable reason, our recent traumatic adventures — which could have conceivably resulted in our deaths — appear to have strengthened that connection. Third, I have seen firsthand the changes in each one of us as a result of being in Reg's presence this summer."

We all murmur our agreement, but Reg waves us off. "You've learned more from each other than you have from me," he says humbly.

"Fourth, during meditation, I have unquestionably experienced physiological changes. And I cannot rule out the role of expanded consciousness in understanding things that cannot be understood with our senses, which," she says with a grimace, "may indicate that there is spiritual energy at work." Before any of us can react, she quickly adds, "In conclusion, while I cannot affirm spiritual energy, I also cannot deny it, and I have come to understand that if I don't fear such uncertainty, perhaps I can embrace it."

A wide smile lights up Reg's face. "On that note," he says, "meditation time." He disappears into the shed and tosses yoga mats out the door. One almost nails Walter on the head, but Free Throw's long arm intercepts it. "Do you want to join us?" he asks Catherine.

I wonder if the Siksika meditate? Catherine accepts a mat. "My grandmother used to sit by the creek for hours," she says, "hearing the wind, the earth and the water." She hesitates, then adds, "She said it was her way of unhearing the voices from the residential schools."

"Your grandmother was a residential school survivor?" I ask. For years, we've heard about the horrors of Indigenous children taken from their parents and culture so that they could be more easily assimilated into the white community. Last year at school, we even had a presentation by a group of First Nation Elders.

Even Reg is taken aback. "Such are the tragic consequences of dualistic thinking." He scrapes some dried dirt off his fingers. "The idea that your belief system must be wrong if mine is right is the dark side of spirituality."

I think about that as I study the painted fireworks. The dark side of spirituality. And yet, it can also reveal light and goodness, even in that moment of darkness. Another paradox.

When Reg continues, it's almost like he's read my mind. "People do horrible things. Yet those same horrific things may start someone on a much-needed spiritual journey. You see, it is often great love or great suffering that does so."

We've all had our share of that lately!

Nikki sets aside her phone. "Which was it for you, Reg? Love or suffering?"

"Both," he tells us. "After Adrianna's death, I was consumed by lost love and guilt. Suicide seemed like a reasonable option, but then a counsellor in prison introduced me to meditation and helped me move beyond fear."

I study the wrinkles on his face and the scars on his forearms as he unrolls his yoga mat. "I still don't quite get how doing nothing helps us get past our fears," I say.

Reg reclines on his mat. "You see, Grady, nothing can either be an empty void or a state of eternal readiness. Meditation just helps us make room to perceive things differently. There are other ways too."

Like Catherine's grandmother's way, I think.

Free Throw plunks down on his mat. "How'd you get to be so wise, Reg?" he asks with awe in his voice.

Reg gives us a sad smile. "I killed a girl," he tells us, and our meditation begins.

As I lie still, I try to silence my mind, but it returns again and again to the realization that Reg has forgiven himself. Finally, I fall into stillness. The chimes ring and I find myself filled with a feeling of hope.

And then Reg drops a bombshell. "I spoke to the police captain this morning."

We hold our breath. To date, nothing has been said about our great adventure from a legal standpoint. For a moment, I picture the five of us sharing a cell and grin. Reg raises one eyebrow at me and I immediately frown.

"Between the four of you, you have managed to break numerous laws and bylaws ranging from driving underage to trespassing to breaking and entering." Catherine starts to protest but Reg silences her. "The good news is that in light of what has transpired, and because you were such a help to the police, all charges have been waived." We exhale in unison. "You do, however, all have to report to the station this Friday at nine a.m. for a debriefing."

Tattoo Girl rolls her eyes, but I know that she is inwardly just as relieved as I am.

"And," Reg adds, "your community service here has been terminated."

Our collective energy sinks. There is no need to ask why but I do anyway. "Why? We belong here. Can't they see how good it is for us?" The others murmur their agreement.

"Actually, they can't," says Reg and even I can understand that.

We sit in silence. Free Throw strokes Walter's coat. Catherine buffs her glasses on her T-shirt, Tattoo Girl traces the lovebirds on her palm, Nikki taps the keys of her phone without typing anything and I just sit. The thought of the

Nothing Club not meeting daily fills me with dread. What will I do without them?

"Where will our new community service assignments be?" asks Nikki.

Reg shrugs. "I don't know. I believe you will be split up and reassigned to other supervisors."

A cloud of discontent settles over us. "So today is our last day here?" I ask. Reg nods. Billy's funeral is Thursday. We'll see each other there, but then . . .

"By the way," says Reg pulling a pamphlet from his pocket. "The diabetes centre is looking for volunteers on Sunday afternoons."

We leap to our feet and in minutes, Nikki has us all signed up for every shift until December.

"Okay," says Reg. "I guess we'll see you Thursday." He looks at us fondly then admires the shed once again. "The Nothing Club," he reads aloud turning to face us with a grin. "They're sure something now, hey Walter?" He meanders towards the pool with the dogs trailing behind him.

We are free for the afternoon, the five of us, five misfits with nothing to do. What will we do? "Let's visit Mrs. Stafford," suggests Catherine. And that is what we do, Nikki filling in Catherine, Free Throw and Tattoo Girl on Reg and Mrs. Stafford's history en route to the hospital.

We enter her room with a cheery hello, ignoring the four-visitor rule. Mrs. Stafford is awake and alert when we arrive. Her IV is gone and she is now on oral antibiotics. "I should be able to go home tomorrow," she tells us. "Then you'll all have to come for lunch."

We glance at each other. Someone has to tell her what's happened, but perhaps that is best left to Reg. "Sure," I reply quickly. "Just let Reg know."

"Let Reg know what?" asks a voice from the doorway.

We all turn and smile at our boss. "I should have known I'd find you here," he says, grinning.

We squeeze him in and half-close the door. Mrs. Stafford's in a private room anyway, so hopefully the nurses won't mind.

"How are you feeling?" asks Mrs. Stafford. "Summer flus are so nasty."

Reg gives us a conspiratorial glance. "Much better, thanks," he replies. "And when you are feeling better, we will give you a full recap of the happenings of the past few days."

"Over lunch," says Mrs. Strafford.

Reg nods and a significant, comfortable silence fills the air. There is nothing to say and nothing to do. I don't have to be psychic to know that nothing is good.

But I linger outside the hospital after the others go. It's one thing to realize that Reg has mastered self-forgiveness, but there's something I need to ask him. "On the farm, in the middle of that gunfight, I felt like my dad was helping me stay calm and make decisions. Was that real?"

"You tell me."

"I-I don't know. He's never done that before." I don't go so far as to ask if Reg thinks this means he might have forgiven me.

Reg looks up at the clouds. "My guess is that your subconscious elicited those memories in a time of great crisis." He squeezes my shoulder. "But I suspect that had more to do with you than your dad, though I can't say for certain."

I scuff my sneaker on the edge of the hospital flower bed and notice the quack grass that threatens to overtake the petunias.

Reg continues. "Grady, I saw the goodness in you the first day you showed up, but you couldn't see it back then. Sometimes we need something dramatic to disrupt our perceptions — or in this case misperceptions."

"It's taken a while," I admit, reflecting on the last five years.

"Yes," agrees Reg, "and sometimes it requires the most unlikely people and circumstances," he continues, "but then that makes us realize that —"

"Everything is connected," I conclude, recalling the quack grass lesson. Only this time I get it!

# EPILOGUE

The buzzer on the stove rings and I slide my shortbread cookies out of the oven. The smell is heavenly. Margaret will love the fact that I hand-cut one in the shape of an antelope. Nikki will tell me how long they take to melt in her mouth and calculate the fat content, and Free Throw will eat incessantly. I close the oven door and place the cookies on a rack to cool. Catherine promised to come help me set up, so I am expecting her first, even though she was the last to join the Nothing Club. Peering through our front window, I watch giant snowflakes drift past twinkling lights onto soft snowbanks. It is perfect Christmas Eve weather!

Mrs. Stafford and Reg are the last to arrive that afternoon. Reg is carrying a giant poinsettia for my mother and Christmas gifts for all of us. It's been a month or so since we've seen him because he went back to the States to see family, but in the interim, we've become venerable experts on educating people about diabetes during our Sunday events.

Reg stands back and looks at each of us, really looks at each of us. "Goodness," he says, "has nothing about the Nothing Club remained the same?"

It's true. We are different, each of us. Margaret has moved from a safe house into an apartment with a roommate. Rigoh is behind bars and she's been in touch with her dad on two occasions. She's now seeing a counsellor on a regular basis. Free Throw towers above everyone at 200 centimetres, but he still doesn't play basketball. He does, however, work part-time at an animal rescue shelter, and there's a new priest at his church that he says sounds a bit like Reg. Nikki, at the counsellor's suggestion, is Tattoo Girl's roommate, but she'll be leaving for Yale University soon. Her apple corer gadget has just recently been patented, she's got two other patents pending and she's investigating the role of quantum physics in spirituality. Catherine is involved with an Indigenous healing circle, and she spends a lot of time at my house when she isn't researching medicinal plants. And I have changed too. I help out around the house more, am taking driving lessons and drop by the fire station occasionally with Charlotte. I still hang out with Will at school . . . but I'm different inside.

The afternoon draws to a close. I stand and raise my glass. "Merry Christmas," I say. "Here's to the Nothing Club."

"Here's to nothing," says Free Throw.

"Nil," adds Tattoo Girl.

"Nought," says Nikki.

"Nix," replies Catherine.

We click our glasses and drink.

As everyone prepares to head out into the snow, Tattoo Girl leans towards me. "You doing okay this Christmas? I know it's a tough time of year."

I think about that. "Yeah," I say. "Yeah, I am."

She gives me a thumbs up, then steps outside to catch a snowflake on her pierced tongue.

That evening, I take Dad's photo and stretch out on

my bed. Charlotte bangs on my door. It's time to open our ritual present on Christmas Eve. I replace the picture on my bureau and head downstairs. My little sister almost bursts with anticipation as she shakes each box and crinkles the crêpe paper within each bag. I choose a rectangular box and open a new pair of ski gloves from Mom. I slide one on, feeling the downy warmth. Charlotte rips open a gift to discover a finger paint set, and Mom opens a set of bath soaps from her sister.

Charlotte is on her feet, still bubbling over with excitement. She dashes off and returns with *The Night Before Christmas*. This is the moment when I head upstairs, flop on my bed and try to forget. Or at least it has been every year since Dad died. She comes to a sudden halt in front of me. "Won't you stay, Grady?" she asks.

I reach for the book. "Only if I get to read," I say as she wedges herself into the chair beside me. Flipping open the cover, I read the inscription:

*To my son, Grady, with love always*
*Dad*

## ABOUT THE AUTHOR

Award-winning Cathy Beveridge has written six young reader books including four historical novels about Canadian disasters and two contemporary hockey novels. After studying English and education at the University of Alberta, Cathy taught for many years and began writing alongside her students. She enjoys gardening, reading, cycling, hiking and spending time with her family. Cathy teaches creative writing at Ambrose University and lives in Calgary, Alberta.